ANNA
and the
ANGEL

ELEANOR WILLIAMS

PARTHIAN

Parthian, Cardigan SA43 1ED
www.parthianbooks.com
© Eleanor Williams, 2024
Print ISBN 978-1-917140-14-0
Ebook ISBN 978-1-917140-15-7
Editor: Gwen Davies
Typeset by Syncopated Pandemonium
Printed by 4edge
Published with the financial support of the Books Council of Wales
British Library Cataloguing in Publication Data
A cataloguing record for this book is available from the British Library.
Printed on FSC accredited paper

ANNA AND THE ANGEL

Eleanor Williams lives in Cardiff, walks with a stick, is a Reader in the Church in Wales, a lawyer in the public sector and an ambassador for Girlguiding Cymru.

For all members of the Adventure Club

The biblical story of Tobias and the Angel doesn't always appear. For instance, you won't find it in a Protestant Bible, but you will find it in Roman Catholic and Eastern Orthodox Bibles. It's a bit like a lighthouse, throwing its beam only occasionally. As well as its not altogether reliable appearance in Bibles, it is very short when you do find it, slotting in between the Old and New Testaments. But if you come across this blink-and-you'll-miss-it story, written a few hundred years before Christ, you'll read a story which goes a bit like this.

Tobit, a pious man, loses his eyesight. His world seems to be falling apart and he prays for death. In a seemingly unrelated incident, at the same time, in a faraway town, a girl called Sarah also prays for death. She is at the end of her tether because every time she marries, her husband dies on the wedding night. And after seven marriages, this is beginning to look 'very much like carelessness'.

God hears the prayers and the angel Raphael is sent to deal with the situation. But, Raphael assumes a disguise. Meanwhile, the Tobit story has moved on. Tobit suddenly remembers he has a lot of money in the safekeeping of a distant relative. He could really do with the money because only his wife is earning. Tobit wants to send his son, Tobias, to retrieve the cash, but the boy is too young to go alone. The angel Raphael, who is now disguised as a man called Azariah, offers to accompany him. They set off, with Tobias' dog.

On their way, Azariah insists on catching and gutting and keeping the innards of a fish. They arrive at Sarah's house. I imagine that by this time, Tobias has stopped trying to make sense of it all. Tobias and Sarah fall in love. It transpires that a malevolent spirit has caused her previous husbands to die. Azariah uses some fish innards to make the malevolent spirit vanish. Tobias and Sarah marry. Tobias does not die on the wedding night and Azariah helpfully collects the money from the distant relative.

Then Sarah, Tobias, Azariah and the dog return to Tobit. All that remains to be sorted out is the issue of Tobit's blindness. Using the remaining innards, Tobias heals his father's blindness.

Occasionally appearing in this tiny book are three women. They're shadowy figures, rarely referred to by name. They are Anna – Tobias' mother; Deborah – Tobias' great-grandmother; and Edna – Sarah's mother.

I wonder what they made of it all? So, what if these women tell a version of the story and leave the men in the background? And what if, instead of happening in the Middle East, it takes place in south Wales? And what if the message of this tiny lighthouse book, refracted through the prism of a different narrator, set in a different location, and in a different time, still shines?

1

Hi Anna,

This isn't about an order from the shop, but your work email was the only way I could see of contacting you. I'm getting in touch because Tobias is here. He's a fine boy: handsome, kind. You and your husband must be so proud of him. He and Az came for supper and are staying the night. And they're very welcome to stay as long as they like. We have plenty of room. I'm not sure why they got off the train at Newport, Tobias said they were making their way to Scotland. But my husband picked them up at the station (Raggy drives a taxi during the day). As he was driving them, they seem to have established that our two families are distantly related – something about your father-in-law and Raggy's mother – and so Raggy brought them home to our house on the outskirts of the city.

They don't actually know I'm writing to you. I hope you don't mind. They were a bit evasive about the nature of their trip. And I understand that it seems to be some sort of boy's own adventure. I hope I'm not treading on toes or betraying confidences, but I thought that if the situations were reversed, I'd want to know.

Kind regards,
Edna.

2

Dear Edna,

Oh! I'm so glad to know the boys are with you – I haven't heard from them since they left and I was getting worried. It's no good talking to T about it – he's completely unconcerned. They're meant to be retrieving money that T left with a relative. I didn't know about their Newport detour, but I'm sure they know what they're doing.

I do want them, well Tobias, to have as much independence as possible. It's been tough for him here, with his dad's illness. I wouldn't have been happy for him making the journey to get the money on his own – he's still quite young for seventeen – but Az turned up from nowhere – T gave him quite a grilling – but he passed – so the adventure begins!

And I totally agree with you – don't let's tell them we're in touch. Please send news, though. And I love to get emails which aren't about work, so this is ideal for me.

Lots of love,
Anna.

3

Hi Anna,

I'm not surprised Az passed your husband's grilling. He'd pass mine! What a specimen! None of us could take our eyes off him as he told a funny story round the supper table last night. We laughed helplessly, and yet now I can't remember what the story was about. I don't think they're moving on today. Raggy made them promise that they'd wait till he got home from work. He's persuaded them to play jazz with him. He's a jazz saxophonist. The taxi driving fills the time between gigs. I'm not going to be around to see the session with Tobias and Az. I'm in the office until late, but I'm sure Sarah, who I think Raggy has talked into singing, will tell me about it.

Your shop looks amazing. I've checked out the website. It's been years since I did any sort of craft, but looking at what your shop sells, I could be converted. I just had to delete a paragraph then. I'd signed off as if this were a work letter, 'if you have any further queries, please do not hesitate to contact me'. Time to go home!

Kind regards,
Edna.

4

Dear Edna,

Thank you so much for your comments about the shop – everything changed when I re-vamped the website – I suddenly found myself with a lot of time on my hands – the boy and I had to come home quite dramatically. We'd been living abroad with T, but he suddenly got worried about the regime that ran the country turning nasty – so I was here and at a loose end. Opening Deborah's physical shop didn't fill all my time – my real job was to build the client base back up – so, to help with this, I decided to re-categorise the website to organise stock by individual crafts (with Tobias' help – he is a good lad) – needlepoint separate from mosaic-making separate from ceramic painting – I'm really pleased with the way it's worked out – sales have taken a bit of a jump and there's been lots of nice feedback. It was actually Tobias' idea to have an 'ideas' section – sort of 'if you like this, you might like to try' – it really worked. I am now doing much more trade online. The only trouble is, I think I prefer seeing customers face-to-face – so I do miss that. It hasn't always been that way – I used to be terrified of customers – you see I never felt that I was supposed to be here – I'd never done any craft – but my in-laws kept a craft shop. It was like an Aladdin's cave – the first time T took me to meet them, after supper at the big table in their kitchen, Deborah, T's grandmother, unlocked a door and we stepped into a darkened shop. She flicked on the light and I gasped. It was wonderful and, funnily enough, I always think of that exact moment of the room being soaked in light as being the time when I fell in love with T.

The shop was stuffed with craft accessories. The walls comprised little drawers filled with sequins, needles, glue pots, pom-poms, crochet hooks, ribbons, tape measures. None of them was labelled, but Deborah seemed to know where everything was. I remember standing that evening behind the long counter with the material measure embedded into its length, ending in the huge gilded, old-fashioned till – looking at the bales of net and sacks of stuffing.

That was the first occasion of many that we women spent in the shop. Those were happy times. I think what I liked was feeling that I was part of a community – Deborah and her world. When the shop was quiet, we'd sit on chairs in the corner and talk. She'd tell me about how, although she was T's grandmother, she'd brought him up. I think she was quite strict – no wonder he has always been so uncompromisingly pious. To be fair, I think that's what attracted me to him initially when he was speaking at a conference I attended. But, she was kind, even if she was strict. It can't have been easy having a couple of newly-weds move in with you. She bought me a little second-hand loom that she set up for me in the shop. If I was there by myself, as I often was after her illness, I'd spend my time making cloth with fantastically coloured bale ends. It was a shrewd move on her part, as I suspect all her moves had been shrewd. Customers used to ask me about it and it made me feel as if the craft business was woven into me.

But, how did the jazz go?

Lots of love,
Anna.

5

Hi Anna,

The jazz was unbelievable. By the time I came home and was re-heating my supper in the kitchen, they were already starting in the music room. Raggy played the sax, and he had persuaded Sarah to sing. Az, it turns out, is an accomplished pianist. He was able to harmonise under the melody superbly, which was just as well, since he didn't seem to recognise pieces by name when Raggy called them out. He wasn't fazed though, he seemed happy enough to follow where Raggy or Sarah were leading. It was amazing that Sarah was taking part at all, she usually wants nothing to do with her father's music. I know this breaks his heart, as they were as thick as thieves when she was little, always singing together on car journeys, 'Puff the Magic Dragon' and 'Sing a Rainbow'.

I have felt ambivalent about the music room since we had it done. It never really got used as it should, I didn't think, until last night. Then, all the details our interior designer had charged so much for, the little tables, the raised dais for the musicians, the subdued lighting really came into their own. Since the arrival of Az and Tobias, things are really falling into place... at last! Have you talked to your husband about how we are related? Oh, that makes me sound so Welsh! Although I am Welsh born and bred, our mania for finding out who's related to whom does make me squirm. But, in spite of that, I am keen to find out. Raggy seems to think it's something to do with a cousin of Deborah's having been related to his grandmother, but he isn't sure. He sets great store by what T thinks as he can remember family stories about what a brilliant boy and young man he was.

Do you correspond a lot by email? I can really hear your voice coming through your letters.

Kind regards,
Edna.

6

Dear Edna,

Ah! A brilliant boy and young man! Those days are long gone, I'm afraid. But I know what Raggy means. That was just how T was when I first knew him. And then Deborah had kept meticulous files of his school reports, certificates, newspaper articles about him – so I feel I have a pretty good idea of what he must have been like as a youngster. But one thing shines through really clearly – he was never motivated by money – he was always doing things for charity – or giving away stuff. I bet his grandmother encouraged this side of him – after all, her own daughter, T's mother, had gone badly wrong with money – the best way of keeping T on the straight and narrow was probably to make sure he wasn't interested in making and acquiring money. Poor Deborah, I think her plan backfired. She can have had no idea about how straight and how narrow T's way was. He was relentless. Of course, by that time I was besotted – so it wasn't until much later that his whole scrimping, self-effacing yet bardic attitude began to irritate me. (And don't even begin to say the 'bardic' bit is a Welsh thing! It's a T thing – trust me – I've witnessed it enough times from him.) Amongst all the tiny mindless acts of selflessness (that never went totally unnoticed, so how mindless can they have been?), he started to develop an interest in seeing that people had proper burials. He began writing prayers, poems and hymns for funerals – he'd work with funeral directors who'd call him late at night, he'd visit bereaved families, he'd raise money for people to have the burial that they'd said they'd wanted. Our house was always awash with the paraphernalia of end-of-life. T always said that people were frightened of death and so didn't deal with it effectively. I don't know. Somehow, he began doing this work on the international stage, and I just couldn't keep up. But, it certainly brought us into the community. After years of rather sterile ex-pat living, we suddenly had friends who'd invite us to parties and share their vivid lives with us. Tobias was starting to be really bilingual. I loved it. But, without warning, T sent us home.

I really don't know where the money came from when we were back. Oh, Tobias and I didn't go short. Deborah had seen to that in her will. But I just worked as many hours as I could in the shop and tried to sustain me and the boy on what I made there. T himself was hardly home. But, I could still feel Deborah and Dai here – willing us to make a success of the shop. I know how wacky that sounds, but I *could*. And it is a nice house, not too far from a park, on a corner, with the shop premises on one of its facades and a deli across the road.... And there's a walled garden behind it with an old apple tree in it – Egremont russets, my favourite – when I saw that tree again when we came back, I knew we'd be alright there, Tobias and I.

T promised that once we'd moved back, it would be easier for him to come and go 'under the radar', so we'd probably end up seeing more of him than when we lived with him. Huh. That didn't happen – I didn't go on about it – I just made the best of it. I did build up a good client base again, and kept trying to imagine how Deborah would arrange the shop as it evolved. I kept going with my weaving in quiet moments. I started to give classes in the evening in the shop. T may not have realised how much I missed being part of a family.

After he'd been away from home for a long time – doing something about end-of-life care, again – oh, and this was just after the regime had been toppled, which seemed to give him more work, not less – he suddenly announced he was returning. By text, would you believe, before he got on a plane! But despite the short notice, Tobias and I made a special effort to welcome him back. I'd appliquéd a Welcome Home banner (for an earlier visit that didn't happen). I found it – miraculously – and hooked it across the front door. Tobias had composed a 'fanfare' on his keyboard for his dad, and I cooked. When he had been away, T had written, talking about a soufflé that I had made before Tobias was born. I could scarcely remember it, and yet, I recalled something about standing expectantly in the kitchen with T's grandmother. I had been trying to peep through the oven door to check it was rising, but Deborah was dismissive of my anxieties. I do remember her explaining briskly that she never transcribed a recipe into her own book unless it was certain to work. So, I retrieved her cookery book from its shelf where it was stored on its side to preserve all the notes about adjusting cooking times, loose pages and recipes torn out of magazines. Cooking from that recipe and awaiting T's arrival, I began to be infused with the older woman's common-sense outlook, so that when T rang the bell, I was feeling well disposed towards seeing him. By the time I got to the door, Tobias had already opened it and Dorcas was jumping up, putting her front paws on T's coat in excitement.

'A dog?' he looked at me, questioningly.

'I'll explain later. We heard Dorcas was going to be put down because her owner couldn't handle her boisterousness. We couldn't say no. Tobias and she have been on a dog training course, and she's much better, except when she gets excited.'

T tousled Tobias' hair and kissed the top of my head in a perfunctory way.

'Can we eat straight away? I'm starving.' I could imagine he was starving, too. He looked like he hadn't eaten properly for months. He slung his travel-stained, sun-bleached rucksack in the hall and deposited his passport in the bookcase where he always kept it. I remember thinking that I'd look inside it later, when the house was quiet, to examine its stamps and try to glean where he had travelled. He wouldn't tell me himself – he said I'd only worry. The boys sat down at the table while the soufflé was in the top oven. I checked that the coq-au-vin was bubbling away below as well as the gratin dauphinois. All T's favourites. And his conversation with Tobias was bubbling away too – school – Scouts – Dorcas. Perfect. I got the feeling that everything, for once, was under control. I lifted the individual souffles to the table and watched them through squinted eyes while T said grace, terrified that they'd sink. But no. And Tobias didn't let on that we didn't usually say grace when it was just the two of us. Phew!

But, then just as we lifted our forks, T's mobile rang. Automatically, without a glance at me, he reached into his pocket and answered it. Its cracked screen glinted in the light of the candles that I'd put on the table. I noticed he studiously looked away from me as he listened, and laughingly said, 'Well, I'm just back. If you'd called half an hour earlier, I'd still have been on the road. No, of course I'll come,' then wrote down a local postcode. After that, still holding the phone to his ear, he just pushed his chair back, did a mock-apologetic grimace, mouthed 'emergency', picked up his coat and car keys from where we always kept them, and disappeared into the night. Tobias and I stayed where we were – transfixed – and then without a word, tucked into our souffles.

Oh – this has turned into a much longer message than I meant – I am sorry. And I haven't really answered your question of how we're related. The truth is, I don't know and I don't want to ask T. And, don't knock how everyone is interested in everyone else, here. When T brought me to Wales, it was a real relief to discover how friendly everyone was. I couldn't believe it. I think it's lovely that I live in a nation of people who seem to believe, deep down, everyone's connected, if only they can find out how.

Right now, I have to open up the shop again for the afternoon. I'll try and write later – and oh, the emails! When we were abroad, Deborah and I used to write to each other constantly. I loved hearing about her world and used to fill up those blue aerogrammes – remember those – with details of trying to get our desert garden to grow, or buying fruit in the market. After she died, I was thrilled to see she'd kept all of my letters in an ottoman in her room. I looked through them – mostly drivel – but I was so touched to see she'd kept them safe. I haven't really written letters since. Not until answering your emails. And I hadn't realised how much I'd missed it.

Lots of love,
Anna.

7

Dear Edna,

Sorry about that. It was just as well I went into the shop and didn't keep writing to you at my laptop on the kitchen table. There must be a local dancing school putting on a show as the shop was full of slightly hysterical mothers. They all seemed to want lengths of satin fabric in different rainbow colours. For a while, the air was filled with the sound of scissors slicing through cloth and half-suppressed sighs as it took time to get each one sorted. Then, once the shop was quiet, I needed to re-order bolts of the fabric. So, apologies. I was talking about the time that T came home and had to go again straightaway, allegedly.

I don't think I've ever been so angry. After Tobias and I had eaten, I tipped the rest of the supper into the bin. I looked at it there, all soggy and useless and I knew how it felt! For the first time ever, I think I came upstairs before Tobias. I just wanted the day to end. Once I had bolted the bedroom door, I went to bed. I always go and kiss Tobias good night, but I couldn't bring myself to that evening – I didn't think I could hold it together and I didn't want to start badmouthing his father to him. I'd grown up with enough of that.

I didn't think I was sleeping, but I must've been because I was startled awake by repeated thumping on the front door. I didn't care how much he knocked, I wasn't opening it. He had to know how angry he'd made me. I felt that this couldn't go on, I couldn't live like this anymore. I got out of bed and sidled up to the window, standing in between the curtain and the window, back to the darkened bedroom. There he was on the pavement, lit up by the street lamp. The harsh white light made him look more cadaverous than ever and somehow, he was the very picture of desperation. I vaguely hoped that none of the neighbours could see him, but frankly I didn't care. I'd had enough of making excuses. He was pushing his hand through his hair and then rubbing his eyes. It was like he was doing some weird dance in the spotlight of the street lamp. This is the trouble – I find him compelling even when I'm cross with him. Then, he moved. I needed to move back a bit myself, to stay hidden. I never usually come this side of the bed. It could do with a dust. I'm ashamed to say that there were spiders' webs hooked between the bed and the window. T was trying the garden gate a bit further up the road. It opened.

Then I lost sight of him. I sneaked out, barefoot (just as well that Tobias couldn't see me now – doing what I forbid him to do) onto the landing, so that I got a good view of the garden. Oh, I hadn't expected that. T was making his way towards the garden shed where there was a light on. He opened the door as quietly as he could. In the cube of light that is released onto the garden, I saw that the garden shed was really very hospitable. Its table had been cleared of tools and there was now a thermos flask on it, surrounded by bulky looking packages of what must have been food. I could make out a hot-water bottle and certainly plenty of blankets – even a pillow. How did all this happen? And then it dawned on me – Tobias. That boy! But, isn't he being exactly the sort of boy that I'd hoped he would be? He's really thought the situation through. He had read the runes. I couldn't help smiling beneath my exasperation – Deborah would be so proud. I tiptoed back to bed and fell asleep straightaway.

I was woken in the morning by Tobias, 'Mum... Mum... Come quickly!'

Pulling on a dressing gown that really I should have thrown away by now and retrieving my bedroom slippers, I made my way blearily downstairs, 'All right... I'm coming... What is it?'

There was a draught blowing in from the open kitchen door. Tobias, who didn't have anything on over his pyjamas, made his way to the shed and was saying something scrambled but in a loud voice. His voice sounded shot through with panic. Perhaps that's why I couldn't make out what he was saying. By the time I reached the shed door, Tobias was already inside with his arm around his father who was crouched on the floor, rubbing his eyes again. T raised his head and looked past me into the garden, 'Is Anna there?'

I swooped down on the floor to cradle him.

And that's it, Edna. There's no more to tell. T is completely blind. There doesn't seem to be an explanation. But I feel so guilty. If I hadn't locked him out, I could have called 999 as soon as he knew there was a problem. We could have saved precious time. Instead of that, he was out there in the cold with fumes from God knows what in the shed. He is very down, and I can't judge what will set him off on a tirade of self-pity. So, I am afraid to ask him how we are related as I think that could unleash more unhappiness. I'm so sorry to be such a wimp, but I do hope you understand.

Lots of love,
Anna.

8

Hi Anna,

What a terrible thing! I can't imagine that you locking T out would have had anything to do with it. I wonder what went on abroad that may have led to it. Has he been to see anyone? Are you getting help? When Raggy asked Tobias how T was, he just answered 'fine'. So, I had no idea. I understand he couldn't possibly go into the trauma of it all when he'd only just met us. Of course, you mustn't ask T about how we are related. I wouldn't want to make things more complicated than they are already. I think our link must be quite remote though, there's nothing more recent than in Deborah's generation.

Tobias talks about his father a lot. I had no idea that he had been away for such a lot of the time. I understand that the boys are on some sort of errand for T. Tobias seems to be very proud of that, and I can understand it, if he is helping his dad. Funnily enough, he was talking about T last night when Raggy offered him a top-up of wine. He refused, saying that he had made a promise to his father not to get drunk. I really don't think a second glass of red wine would have got him drunk but it shows that he is never far from his thoughts. Raggy asked what else his dad had said. Tobias said something really interesting: that he had told him to bear in mind what he hates, and never to do that to anyone else. There was silence round the table. We've never said anything like that to Sarah, and I think it's a pity. Because it struck me that it was a really workable, sensible piece of advice to give. Perhaps because Tobias could see that we were really listening, he kept going with the pieces of advice that T had given him. I liked the bits about being circumspect in all the things he does. All seventeen-year-olds should be told that! Oh, but I must tell you about one bit that was really sweet. Tobias started explaining about how T told him that he should marry someone who fits in with his family, someone who has the same outlook as he does, not someone who has different values. At one point he caught Sarah's eye, and then was too embarrassed to go on, so drank some of his second glass of wine!

And I am delighted to be the cause of your writing letters again. When I mentor people at work, the process gives me the same satisfaction as I feel now. Maybe that's why Raggy and I are still married? We are not in similar worlds, but maybe we mentor each other. We probably have the same values.

Kind regards,
Edna.

9

Dear Edna,

Would you tell me about Sarah please? And I realise I've been going on about myself and not asking you about you at all. Where is your office? What do you do?

I'm just waiting for a fruit crumble to finish cooking – T has not lost interest altogether in food, though he's not moving about much. So, he's putting on weight – I do worry. My next door neighbour is a Pilates instructor and has offered to do keep fit sessions with T, but he's not having any of it. He just sits in a manky old chair in his room, all day, just thinking. And he wears the same jogging bottoms and sweatshirt day after day. When I suggest changing them, he shrugs. I look at the steep gradient of his shoulders, his body silhouetted like a boulder against the dark muddle of the room around him and leave quietly, keeping the door open so I can hear him should he call, wishing I had the crampons and ropes to reach him. His mobile used to ring non-stop in the first days, but I don't know if he's forgotten to charge it, or leaves it turned off or whether people have stopped trying to ask him favours. But it's silent up there now. I took a radio upstairs, but T wouldn't even let me plug it in. He said that he had no interest in a world he could not be part of. I'm glad Tobias is away from it all. I'm ashamed to say that my escape is the shop, which bizarrely seems to go all the better the more grim it is at home.

I do look forward to hearing from you, Edna.

Lots of love,
Anna.

10

Hi Anna,

My job – that's easiest. I'm a partner in a law firm working in a shiny office building with an improbable roof in town. Mostly employment law work acting for the employer. So that means that when a firm wants to make redundancies, or discipline one of their staff, or hear a grievance, I get involved. It's not creative, not fulfilling, not energising, but I have some nice colleagues and it pays the bills. Oh, and it means I have a nice car and nice clothes. God, that sounds shallow! But, honestly, it makes me happy. Is that pathetic? I knew when I met Raggy what the trade-off would be: I'd keep a roof over his head, and he'd keep me sane.

I don't know that I'd ever really wanted children. I was enjoying fine wine, exclusive hotels and lie-ins, but then Sarah came along. I needn't have worried because really, my life went on pretty much undisturbed. Without us ever discussing it, Raggy took over most of the childcare duties. I remember looking at my watch one evening in the office and thinking if I rushed home, I'd make bath time. But then I thought that Raggy would do it better than I would anyway, so I kept working. I think really there have only been two lasting consequences of this:

1.   I'm not particularly close to Sarah. But then, a lot of mothers aren't close to daughters.
2.   There are very few of Sarah's childhood photos with me in them. Instead, it's all Raggy and Sarah at the piano, at the park, dressed up for Hallowe'en.

Raggy is fiercely loyal when we all go for family therapy. He talks about how I let him have full rein in bringing up Sarah. I smile benignly, but I do squirm. Why, you ask, are we going for family therapy? Do you see how I've chattered on and managed to avoid the crux of the issue? And I will tell you, only now I can hear the boys coming in. It sounds like they're lugging equipment. I'd better see if I can go and help (by that I mean if I can pour anyone a drink).

Thank you for listening, Anna. I think I'm off-loading because we've never met and yet you feel close. You could be charging thousands for this!

Kind regards,
Edna.

11

Dear Edna,

Take your time. There is no rush at all. I've been thinking a lot about time recently. In the kitchen (why can I never get the work surfaces clear?), there's a window above the sink which looks out onto the garden. I'm proud of the garden. It was a wilderness when we arrived, it had run to seed when the house was empty after Deborah's death, but I have managed to make it interesting and cottagey again, clearing its hidden seats and sinuous paths. Of course, there wasn't money to spend on it, but I think it's almost more interesting for that. Anyway, what was I saying about time? Yes, I watch the garden changing seasons, the unbelievable spring green moving to that comfortable brown of autumn which I seem to like more the older I get. It makes me realise that time is artificial, really. We divide it into minutes and hours and days, but the reality of what happens, happens irrespective of time. It strikes me that things aren't really sequential ever, they're much more random than that. I think that about T's blindness – all those years when he wasn't here – and then the days now where he might as well not be here and he doesn't really want to be here, either. One block of time doesn't seem to be related to the other. I'm not sure if I'm making much sense. But what I want to say is: take your time. There is no rush to tell me more about Sarah. I'll wait.

Lots of love,
Anna.

12

Hi Anna,

Thank you for understanding. Although I'm not sure how much of the following anyone can understand, given that I don't understand it myself. When she was about sixteen, boys started being interested in Sarah. I was inclined to be very strict, but Raggy had a much more laid-back attitude. So, we got used to having a procession of boys coming to supper and then, because they all seemed to be in bands, spending the evening in the music room with Raggy and Sarah. So far so good, I thought.

I distinctly remember the first time there was an incident. I was loading the dishwasher: I can't bear clutter – especially dirty dishes – and Raggy sauntered into the kitchen. As I closed the door and pressed the switch of the machine, Raggy put his arm around my waist, and said softly, 'I've left them to it.'

'What do you mean, left them to it?'

'Nothing.... Stop panicking. I don't mean anything, except that Neil is trying out a song he's written, and Sarah seems to be harmonising in the chorus. You really should relax, Ed. I think it's great that Sarah can begin to socialise more with people of her own age in a safe, supportive environment.'

Then, we heard a scream from the music room. It was Sarah's voice crying for help. Even then, I didn't realise how serious it was. I even think I might have joked about a safe and supportive environment as we made our way towards the noise. By the time we reached the room, Sarah was distraught. She was standing with her hands inside the sleeves of her sweatshirt and shaking her head. She was looking down at Neil who was lying on the floor.

'I thought he was just trying to frighten me, Mum, but it's not a joke. I can't feel a pulse.'

Raggy comforted Sarah while I knelt down. I could smell Neil's aftershave and as I held his hand, I remember noticing how clean his nails were. This evening had really meant a lot to him. There was nothing to be done. The lad was dead. We phoned the emergency services, and Neil's parents. After everyone had left the house and the sobbing had subsided, Raggy and I went through the evening again with Sarah. The story didn't change. Neil hadn't banged his head, hadn't complained of any pain, he just collapsed.

Of course, we went to the funeral. I remember how, in the cold chapel that smelt alarmingly of gas, everyone made a fuss of Sarah, sympathising and commenting on what a shock it must have been. There was still no explanation, but Sarah seemed buoyed up by the goodwill of all the young people filling the crematorium. I didn't think she'd taken it too badly at all. It was a horrible thing to have happened, but she is a sensible girl.

When the same thing happened six more times – yes six! – people began to be much less kindly disposed to Sarah. I mean, not exactly the same thing happened. One lad was mowing the lawn, I remember. He said he had always wanted to try a sit-on lawnmower. We were all there for that one. He had finished mowing and was handing the keys back to Raggy. We were giving him a round of applause and suddenly he went. Just fell down. One lad was in Sarah's room with her. By now she was twenty-one and Raggy and I were hopeful that he would be the one. Sarah's therapist worked so hard with her to get her to not feel guilty. Sarah thought she was killing all these boys. Anyway, Raggy and I had loitered downstairs for as long we could, and we were just getting into bed and the screams came. Raggy nodded his head wearily before reaching for his dressing gown.

For what it was worth, the paramedics were unfailingly nice. Every time, they reassured us that we hadn't been to blame in any way at all, that Sarah was, in some ways, a victim along with these boys. It's understandable though that they began to be less sympathetic than they had been at first. After leaving school, Sarah chose a college course which meant she could stay at home. Who can blame her? The media had already picked up on the predicament. Snooping reporters with long lenses published some cruel stuff, making her out to be less than innocent. I wanted to take them on, and Raggy and I even had meetings with the media lawyer at work, but Raggy persuaded me to let it go. It was Sarah's welfare that was paramount, he said. By this point, you can imagine she was so fragile that having the pressure of a court case would have just been too much.

So, there we are. If you google any of us, this is what comes up. I was surprised that you have kept writing to me. Most people keep their distance. And we carry on. Sarah with her interior design, Raggy with his jazz, where his colleagues are more like a supportive family, and co-workers, and me in the office where I try to keep client contact to a minimum. And always use my maiden name.

Look, Anna, I understand if you don't want to keep in touch with me. I can easily speak to Tobias and Az to tell them that they're needed back home as soon as possible. Do let me know what you think. I really understand how odd this all is.

Kind regards,
Edna.

13

Oh, dear Edna,

That must have been dreadful for all of you. I have been turning
it over as I have got on with my weaving. The clack clack of the
shuttle going back and forth was like a metronome: I almost
feel like I've been listening to the cadences of your troubles.
Sometimes, I hear a single piercing note which I imagine to be
a yowl of anguish from Sarah, and sometimes I hear muffled
low notes which I imagine to be you and Raggy talking in
whispers. When T used to notice what I was doing and had
listened to me talking about weaving, he'd say that the way I
connected the colours in my loom with music was batty, but
that he loved me for it. He doesn't say that any more but I
still almost hear sounds when I weave. Somehow, writing that
down does seem batty. I know what he was going on about.

I have been worrying about the boys imposing on you by
being there, and I can't see any sign of them moving on, or
getting the money for T. But now I wonder, without wanting
to presume, if they are, I don't know, needed in some way. Are
they helping to cheer Sarah up at all? Of course, I don't want
them to come home yet. I wouldn't dream of saying that! As
I was weaving meditatively yesterday, I had a funny sensation

that Az and Tobias visiting may help to start to unravel your worries. Almost like undoing a knot, breaking a cycle, stopping a loop carrying on turning. I expect *you* think I'm batty now!

Lots of love
Anna.

14

Hi Anna,

I was very afraid that you wouldn't want to keep writing after
the oddness of our story. But you are right about something
being unravelled; gosh, things had been knotted tightly. Do
you know, I used to think it was all my fault. Raggy had been
engaged to someone else when we met and I'm afraid I was
rather ruthless. I thought that the situation now was payback
time. But, the atmosphere is completely different here since
Az and Tobias have arrived. It's lighter, somehow. I know what
you mean about there being a link between the two families.
Of course, we are related in some way or other, but I feel there
is a more immediate connection than that. Something to do
with my Sarah and your T. In a funny way, their situation is
similar: they're each desperate. I must admit that I hadn't
realised how desperate Sarah was until a fortnight ago. It was
Tuesday, which is the day the cleaning lady, Margaret, does
upstairs – thank goodness. She had gone suddenly into Sarah's
room and found her standing on the bed trying to throw a long
scarf over the light fitting. She hadn't heard Margaret coming
in, and it wasn't till she heard her name called quietly that
she looked down. Margaret has known Sarah since she was

tiny. She used to be a secretary in work, but she was hopeless. I phoned her up at home on the day she was dismissed and asked whether she might be interested in coming in to clean temporarily for me until she got herself sorted. That was over twenty years ago. I think we pay her over the odds, which does worry me. But then she is very loyal and is always careful with Raggy's instruments. Those are both priceless qualities in a cleaning lady, I think. Anyway, Margaret didn't need to ask Sarah what she was up to. She told me later that both of them had sat on the bed. She put her arm around Sarah who cried and cried and said how hopeless she felt. We'd probably have been better off getting Margaret in at the start of all this, rather than paying for expensive counselling! Sarah promised her never to try anything like that again. I believe Sarah will stick to her word. And then the boys arrived, and now the incident with the scarf and the light fittings seems so remote.

Talking of the boys, how much do you know about Az? I can't help feeling he's central to the connection between our two families, but I can't work out why. I've tried to talk to Raggy about this, but he is so pleased to see Sarah happier than she has been for ages, that he is no help at all. Every time I've tried to talk to Az himself, he gives amusing answers to my questions, making me forget what I'd been asking. He did say that Tobias got in touch with him online and that he's involved in international development. He plays the jazz piano beautifully, but is evasive about where he learned. Tobias mentioned that Az knew a lot of T's relatives, which made me wonder if we are related to him in some way. I'm even starting to think he looks familiar. Is it just a middle-aged fantasy on my part? How much do you know about him? We have a private detective in the criminal department at work, and I could ask him to make some enquiries if you're interested. Let me know.

Kind regards,
Edna.

15

Dear Edna,

The awful thing is that I don't really recollect meeting Az for the first time. I was busy in the kitchen when Tobias trailed through and Az went in after him. I have a vague memory of turning round and nodding to him. We didn't shake hands or anything. I have a sense that I was doing something at the sink and so my hands would have been dirty. I pointed the way upstairs with my head and the boys went to T's room. I shouted after them, 'Knock before you go in, boys. Oh, and if T wants anything brought down once you've finished, could you bring it? It would save me a trip.'

I wouldn't know what had gone on in that room if Tobias hadn't told me. It must just have struck him as fairly extraordinary, or he wouldn't have bothered commenting. I imagine the boys opening the door to T's room. The stench of what I always think of as futility in that room is something I find repulsive. It's not dirty – I make sure of that, but there is a smell of hopelessness that is overpowering. T would have been sitting in his chair with his back to the window. The curtains would have been drawn, bringing the room into shadow. The mound of a single bed with crumpled clothes perpetually piled on it takes up the length of one wall.

According to Tobias, Az seemed to gleam with special brightness in that context. I could tell he was embarrassed to be saying that to me, but I know what he means – there is a gleaming quality to Az, as if he's not been sullied by the world, somehow. He seems like he is newly out of his box. Tobias was also struck that although, for him, this was a tense interview – T would decide if Tobias and Az could go travelling, Az didn't appear to be nervous at all. He wasn't casual, though. He was respectful and formal to T, calling him 'sir'. How did he know that would please T immensely? This must have put T at his ease because the interview – and he would have given Az a grilling – must have gone well. T was really fixated on the business about where Az was from. T's very keen on who belongs to whom, I think it's a throwback from Deborah. Apparently he asked Az 'Who are your people?'

Tobias said he shuffled awkwardly as his father got onto his conversational hobbyhorse. But Az remained still, with his eyes fixed on T as if he were decoding him there in the smelly twilight of the room. He answered T jokingly, 'Are you hiring me or my family?'

How did he know that T would have loved that? There is nothing better that Az could have done than show T that he wasn't frightened of him. Tobias looked on, intrigued, by all accounts. He had never seen anyone deal with his father like that before, and he was in awe of someone who seemed to be laughing – not at T, but at the whole situation – as if he was just going through the pleasantries, but really knew how it was all going to turn out.

'No, but seriously,' Az continued, 'I do understand why you want to know a bit about me. My name is Azarias. My father was Ananias, which I think means that we are related.'

T was gobsmacked and could barely get his words out. He spluttered, 'Well, of course I knew Ananias as well as his brother Jonathas. The three of us worked together on many a project. Good boys both of them, but then of course their father, Samaias, was a great man. He must have been your grandfather, then. Well, well, well... What a turn of events. And to think I was worried about letting Tobias go and get this money with someone I'd never met. Then it turns out to be you! I haven't thought about those boys for years, not since they moved away. They both well?'

'Quite well. Thank you for asking, sir.' Az's voice smiled out of the dark.

Now, I never heard about Ananias and Jonathas before. Or maybe I had just forgotten. But it would have been churlish to bring up a little detail like that. T seemed happy and if he was happy then I was happy. After that time, T was always exasperated if I expressed concern about Tobias. He placed complete trust in Az, even saying to me generously once, 'You will see him return with your own eyes!' After he said that, I didn't like to keep on. What T would have given to have seen with his own eyes! And yet, as far as Az was concerned, he seemed to have more insight than me.

So you see, Edna, that's all I know. I can't imagine that helps you much.

Lots of love,
Anna.

16

Hi Anna,

I'm really anxious that you might be cross. Let me explain. I took the details from your last letter about Az's background and asked the private detective used by work to have a look at them. I was just so curious. Az seems very familiar to me, somehow: I suppose I was hoping to be able to surprise everyone with some nugget of information. Nothing. This detective, usually so successful in every case he takes on, turned up nothing. He said he had conned all his usual sources and he found Az's father, uncle and grandfather, but no record of Az himself. Of course, it's not conclusive, and I am sure that Az would not lie, but it is interesting. Please don't be cross with me for having gone ahead and searched without you expressly saying I could.

I do have some news for you, though. It's about a fish. I don't think you'll know about this because the fish incident seems to have happened in between the boys leaving your home and arriving here. I'm not quite sure what it's all about yet, and I remember them mentioning it when they arrived, but it wasn't until last night that they told the whole story.

It started with a discussion of markets. We were talking

about what markets we liked. Raggy was explaining how he visited the bazaar in Istanbul when he was inter-railing as a young man and still remembers the spices, carpets, coloured plates. Ever since, he has been disappointed by every other market he had ever seen. Sarah gave a spirited defence of Newport market, mostly because as a young child she had enjoyed sitting on the statue of a pig at the market entrance. But then Az started to talk. He had been intrigued, he said, by Cardiff market. He described the cheese shop, the coffee shop where you stand glugging an espresso before going on your way. He even waxed lyrical about the great carcasses of meat suspended overhead and the stalls selling flowers. His favourite, though, was an umbrella shop. He said he didn't know that such a thing existed and then enumerated the varieties of umbrella he'd seen there – telescopic, fancy, see-through, brown. He went on and on about it in a way that made me wonder if he'd never been into a market before. But I didn't say anything. Sarah asked why he'd gone there. It was then that he and Tobias explained, each chipping in to the story, that they'd needed to buy a fish there. There's a good fish stall at the back of the market. Of course, Az was enthralled by it. He'd known exactly what sort of fish he wanted. Tobias remarked how Az had commented on the speckled belly of the particularly fresh specimen the stallholder had held up. Then Az asked the fishmonger to make three separate packages. One for the heart and liver of the fish, one for the gall and the other for the remainder. Tobias thought they'd better pay extra for a chiller bag as they were on their way to the station to get the train to Scotland. He himself didn't seem to know why they were buying the fish but was contented that Az would explain once they were on their way. I suppose that, once T said he was happy with Az, then there was no need for anyone else to worry too much.

Once they got outside the market, Az asked Tobias to open the chiller bag. He took the small package of the remainder of the fish out and put it in a bin. He offered no explanation about why he'd done this, but just smiled. Almost the first thing they did once they'd come here, after introducing themselves, was to ask if they could put their packages into the freezer. So that's where they are now. Do you know what they'd want with the innards of the fish? Again, Az wasn't forthcoming when he was asked why, last night. He simply answered, with a sheepish grin, 'I think they'll come in handy, that's all.'

Now you can see why I am so intrigued about him.

Kind regards,
Edna.

17

Dear Edna,

A fish! No, that was not something they mentioned before leaving here. I wonder what they are up to? Will you keep me posted? Another mystery is that the private detective couldn't trace Az. I suspect that it's not a mystery at all, but rather my having misheard the names of his father and uncle. And, of course I'm not cross with you for having taken the initiative like that! I wish I had access to those kinds of networks instead of sitting here weaving and seeing the occasional customer.

But, at least it gives me time to think. And I have been thinking of how I answered you when you asked me about Az – I said that I hadn't really seen him, but that he just passed through the kitchen on his way to see T. Well, that is factually true, but perhaps not your 'truth, the whole truth and nothing but the truth'. When I looked round from the sink and saw Az in the kitchen, I felt totally seen, absolutely known. Does that sound strange? I imagine it's the sensation that people refer to when they talk about, 'love at first sight', but I wasn't aware of a romantic emotion. I just felt that Az knew where I had been, what I was going through and where I was heading. I think I may have grasped this as rivulets of water were running down my elbows. I must have seemed stunned, involuntarily clutching the dripping dishcloth. Looking as he does, I suspect he gets this all the time and so might not have noticed anything strange. It's a relief to me that T likes Az so much. It means that I haven't needed to examine too closely how I feel about him. I wonder if T could see Az, would he like him so much? Maybe not. T has a sort of distrust of people who are too beautiful. I think that's why he married me!! I think he imagines that beautiful people have a life that is just too easy! And that goes against his activist nature. If people are beautiful, how likely are they to be an underdog? And how can you fight for them if they're not an underdog?

Oh, talking of dogs, how is Dorcas? I do miss her yapping. She's a bit of a picky eater, but I'm sure Tobias will have helped you find a variety of food that will keep her interested. Funnily enough, biscuits never seem to fail with her.

Lots of love,
Anna.

18

Hi Anna,

Dorcas adores Sarah. She sleeps on Sarah's bed and they are seldom seen out of each other's company. As for feeding her, Sarah sees to that, after being inducted into the mysteries by Tobias. Margaret is mostly to be found in the kitchen; she and Sarah have always been close and so between them they make sure that Dorcas has plenty to eat. I don't know what Sarah will do when Dorcas goes. Thank goodness, there's no sign of Az and Tobias moving on – sorry, Anna. The jazz they play with Raggy is getting really good and they even persuade Sarah to sing with them sometimes. Last night, Raggy was talking about recording some tracks with the boys. So, it doesn't seem like a move is imminent. I was thinking about this as I drove to work today and it struck me that the boys don't seem to show any concern for getting the money back from T's relative. Is there anything I can do to help here? I'm sure it's the sort of issue that my firm could handle very easily. What do you think? I know it can be sometimes delicate when it's a question of money between family members, but perhaps that's the reason why we could help. I dread the thought of you and T waiting for a cheque and the boys just whiling away their time here, playing jazz. Will you let me know?

Kind regards,
Ed.

19

Dear Edna,

I am hopeless with money. I've always left that to T, and in the shop, I've always used an accountant. So, I am not really able to shed much light on the money that the boys are trying to recover. But, here's what I've been able to piece together...

As a cover for his philanthropic work – and once Tobias and I were back home, safe and sound – T ingratiated himself with the regime. He worked his way up until he became what is known as a purveyor for the Cabinet. This was a good ploy because the regime never suspected that he was working for an authority other than them. Of course, they were vaguely interested about when people were buried – after all, they wanted to keep their skulduggery covered, so funnily enough they were helpful in ensuring that T's work in this regard was kept under wraps. I think he felt that by burying people promptly (which was important to their loved ones, but not particularly to the regime – they were more concerned about killing them in the first place), he was taking a stand against the regime. It was his act of defiance, his mark of resistance – burying properly, communicating locations accurately and recording meticulously.

I never really understood what a purveyor did. But, it

seems to have involved doing whatever needed to be done. I suspect that what the Cabinet needed to be done was not always strictly legal, although I have no evidence of that. All I do know is that T earned a lot of money at that time. My experience of working in the shop is that you don't earn a lot of money unless you show some flair and take some initiative. Which leads me to think that T must have known how to bend the rules, at least. He received a lot of his wages in cash and he ended up with a large sum of silver. This would have been a problem. Not only would he have had to explain where it came from, but he would also have to explain how the cabinet had paid tax in giving it to him. So, he left it for safekeeping with a man called Gab. I think they buried it together. As far as I can understand, T seems to have given the boys the coordinates for where this money is. There is probably no other record of the money. I remember, way back, T having received a letter from Gab's brother to say that the regime had caught up with Gab. It had always been a joke that they'd called Gab 'Gab the Gob' because of his taciturn nature. I think it's very unlikely that Gab would have spoken to anyone about the location of the money, unless he told the regime under torture, but I think they'd have had bigger fish to fry. So, as long as the coordinates are accurate, I don't see that there will be any problem about retrieving the money.

The slightly odd factor is that T had forgotten all about this buried cash. And for my part, I didn't think of it. I remember T saying soon after he had decided what to do with it, that it was just as well he had buried it. The regime was always unstable and he'd had to leave his job as purveyor in a hurry. He needed to lie low for a while (which was when he came back to us). He brought nothing with him – all his assets were seized while he was still there – and he had to rush to get out. T couldn't go and retrieve the buried cash at that stage – he was afraid we were being watched as enemies of the regime. Of course, when the danger was over, the cash had been forgotten about. I think how handy it would have been to have all that money after T became blind. I used to lie awake at night, worrying about how we would make ends meet – if we needed to sell the house, whether Tobias would be able to carry on in education or whether he would have to pack in his studies and earn a living.

T and I were sitting, listening to the radio one afternoon. I didn't want the noise of my weaving to interrupt our listening and so I was getting on with a bit of embroidery, I remember. He had been very quiet throughout lunch – I was glad that he couldn't see how the house was beginning to look grubby and the garden, through the window, was looking unkempt. Everything seemed grey that day. One of those comedies came on the radio. You know, the ones with the canned laughter. They can seem unbelievably tragic when you're not in the mood for a comedy. That must have been why I'd got up to turn the radio off. Anyway, one character, a drifter, as I recall, was called Gab. Just as the comedy seem to be reaching its climax, with Gab having muddled up place settings at a wedding and inadvertently caused comic mayhem, T suddenly raised his head and said quite quietly, 'Gab the Gob!'

That meant nothing to me, but slowly, in the fresh silence of the room, T began to recount the story of this buried silver. He had memorised the map coordinates and he made me write them down there and then – in fact, I embroidered them into the work on my lap. It was only when we talked over this afterwards, with Tobias, that fragments of the original story came back to me. So, I think it's true. I think I've heard this before. I hope against hope that the money is there. T has promised to pay very generous wages to Az, on the basis that they do find the money. If they don't, then we are in serious trouble. But I'm not going to think about that. I'm sure T's got this all right. So that's all I know about the money. It's a bit pathetic isn't it, how sketchy my knowledge is? I really must try and get a grip of financial matters.

Lots of love,
Anna.

20

Hi Anna,

You are funny! There's nothing to understanding money at all. I think you would enjoy getting to grips with it. Perhaps when you and I can reveal that we have been in touch for this time, I can visit you and maybe do a bit of a financial awareness workshop with you. What d'you think? In return, I could do with some tips on how I can encourage Sarah.

Seeing her with Az and Tobias makes me realise how I have ignored her. As soon as she showed no aptitude for doing the sort of work I do, or being interested in winning, I left her to her own devices. Then, when we started to have problems with young men, I distanced myself even more; I left her to Raggy, just as I did when she was little. That's a horrible thing to have to realise. But, in spite of me, she's flourishing now. Az and Tobias include her in conversations, take notice of her preferences. I get the sense she's really unfolding in their presence. And Raggy looks on, smiling beatifically, as if he always knew that Sarah would blossom into that sort of woman. You can hear it in her singing. She stays silent and listening while the three of them play, and then from out of nowhere she starts singing a note that seemingly has nothing to do with the music they are playing, but instantly blends to their melody. Raggy thinks she has a real gift.

She has always been too self-conscious to sing, which I could never understand. She can sing, so why not sing? Raggy was more tolerant; but I know how hurt he was. The fact that she has started to participate in these jazz sessions seems to be part of the same pattern that started just before the boys arrived. I had a sense that something was unlocking when lots of art-related deliveries arrived. When I passed her room, I could see that she had set it all up near the window; I'm glad about this. She has a lovely room with huge picture window at one end. I paused in the corridor outside her room and was in two minds whether I wanted to deal with a conversation that was bound to be awkward at best, and at worst, confrontational. But I did knock the door which was ajar and Sarah called me in.

'What are you doing?'

'I'm painting, Ed.'

'That's lovely, darling, I used to love the art you did in school. I remember the programme cover you did for *The Gondoliers*. We've still got that somewhere, I must track it down.'

'Ed, I'd really like to get on with this. Unless you had anything particular you wanted to say, is it okay if we talk about it at supper?'

'Oh, that's clever! You're using the window to frame the painting! Brilliant! But are you quite sure you want to make the colours as vivid as that? The lawn is almost a lime green and the gravel drive is sparkling. Is it quite right, darling?'

'I'm not taking a photo of it, Ed. This is how it looks to me. I was sitting on my bed yesterday, looking out of the window and the rain suddenly stopped. Everything seemed so calm and hopeful. It was as if something nice was coming down the drive towards the house, something that would change everything. I made sketches with stuff I had lying around, but I knew exactly what colours and textures I wanted. And that's what I'm doing. Would you mind leaving me to it?'

And I did. Tiptoeing quietly out of her room as if I didn't want to rouse her demons, now that they are obviously asleep and letting Sarah create.

Kind regards,
Edna.

21

Dear Edna,

Does Sarah call you Ed? I do like that. It means that you can be real friends, being on first name terms. Having said that, Tobias has always called me Mum and I must say, I do love it. I felt as if I'd been made into someone new at his birth, just because I had a new name. Tobias' birth was a new beginning for me. I remember Deborah telling me that. She would have been so interested in Sarah's painting.

I've never felt inspired to paint; my creativity needs trammelling, somehow: weaving's perfect for me. That old lady was a great painter, though. When the craft shop was hers, she had space for a studio cum gallery, upstairs. Now, I'm ashamed to say, it's a cluttered store room. She specialised in still lives, but I used to joke with her that they seemed anything but still. The objects Deborah painted seemed to have a life of their own. I used to love her spring flowers – they were not just flowers, but emphatic announcers of a new start. She catalogued everything she painted, and by the end of her life, her paintings were getting to be quite valuable. I haven't been as assiduous as I could have been with making sure that Deborah's legacy is preserved, although T and I have a lot of her paintings round the house. But, of course, it's no good mentioning anything about his grandmother's paintings to T now. It would only unleash a train of bitterness that he can't see them. I find myself glimpsing at them, almost furtively. I do derive huge comfort from seeing them, it's like looking at Deborah again. She would be delighted to hear of Sarah's renewed enthusiasm for art. Perhaps, when we can tell them that we know each other and have been in correspondence for all this time (and it does seem like 'all this time', although what is it – weeks?), Sarah would consider designing some cards that I could sell in the shop? Why does that seem such a daydream? I suppose because there are so many hurdles to get through first – the money, the blindness, Sarah's future. But it's important to have daydreams, isn't it?

Lots of love,
Anna.

22

Hi Anna,

Hearing you explain about Deborah's painting so generously and so truthfully makes me ashamed. Because I haven't been totally honest with you about Sarah's story. Probably, this added twist in her narrative won't make that much difference – not the facts, at least. But as I get older and see more, I wonder what use facts by themselves are. And there I am, in my office-life, prizing facts above everything else. Oh dear, I'm not making much sense, I'll just tell you this bit.

When Sarah was a little girl, about three, she developed an imaginary friend. We thought this was quite sweet at the time. It was just when we were thinking about (never seriously, from my point of view at least) having a second child. Initially we thought that Sarah was just sensing a fault line and trying to drive home the point about wanting a sibling. I'm not sure, though, that at three she could realistically have done this. This imaginary friend started quite innocently. But here's the strange thing, his name was As – short for Asmodeus, she said (where did she get that name from?). Sarah started to mention his name when we'd ask her who she'd seen that day in nursery. Then, As became something more like a scapegoat.

When there was felt tip on the wall, or crusts of bread thrown surreptitiously under the breakfast bar, Sarah would always claim, wide-eyed, 'As did it!'

Raggy and I didn't take this very seriously. Perhaps we should have. But you know what kids are like. We wouldn't hear anything of As for a while, and then there'd be milk spilt on the kitchen floor or an upturned toybox and again, 'As did it!' would be the explanation.

I did start to get worried when this situation progressed. Sarah started owning up herself to the misdemeanours, but when we asked her why she'd done something, her explanation would be 'As made me do it'.

For some reason, I found this more sinister than Sarah simply plonking the blame on an imaginary friend. Suddenly, the imaginary friend was more difficult to be reckoned with, if he could direct Sarah's moves. The most serious incident came when Raggy and I had been getting the house ready for an evening do for some important client. These clients had mentioned to me that they liked jazz, and so Raggy had put together a little group of some really good musicians. We'd been tidying the house frantically, there were caterers everywhere, Margaret had been brought in to help and she was run off her feet. Suddenly, someone – Raggy probably – noticed that Sarah didn't seem to be anywhere about. I told everyone to stop what they were doing and search. After a while of us screaming Sarah's name, one of the caterers noticed a little girl sitting on the garage roof. I have no idea how Sarah got up there. And I don't know why she had gone. Predictably, all she would say was 'As made me do it'.

Even Raggy was cross with her that day. I think he managed to get through to Sarah how worried she was making us, because we didn't hear any more about As for years after that. In fact, he only came back again when our recent problems began. I distinctly remember driving to the first funeral, and Sarah's voice from the back of the car, talking almost to herself, 'I wonder will As be there?'

I looked at her in the rear-view mirror, her face was pinched and she was absolutely genuine. Her question had been very real to her, even though it made no sense to me and Raggy. Raggy leaned over and touched my shoulder, and I understood that he thought it was better not to pursue anything with Sarah. So, I let it go.

As kept reappearing, in oblique ways like that, and each time it happened, I wasn't really sure if Sarah was aware she was mentioning him. I don't think Sarah ever mentioned him in therapy. It's almost like she doesn't talk about him voluntarily. He exists, if he exists, in her subconscious childhood mind. I have wondered over the years what he looked like. When Az came into our kitchen with Tobias, I wondered if I'd found out.

Kind regards,
Edna.

23

Dear Edna,

Tobias never had an imaginary friend. I kept hoping one would appear; I would look out for the signs and quiz him if he mentioned names of people in nursery. They always seem to have a factual basis, though. He always seemed very grounded, perhaps too grounded, like T. This is why I'm glad he's having an adventure, although he's only in Newport! But you know what I mean. Life is opening up for him, and it's not all just predictable and childlike.

My life is the same. T is no better. If it wasn't for Judith next door (and you as well, now!), I don't know that I'd talk to anyone. It was when I was chatting to her yesterday afternoon that I had a memory of Deborah that I think is quite telling. Judith asked me where I would live, if I could live anywhere. I was surprised by the immediacy of my response. Paris, I said, definitely Paris. She asked me if I'd ever been there and I said yes, with Deborah. Her craft shop bought ribbons from a specialist seller in Paris. I remember a dark narrow shop near a railway station. The lady who kept it, Madame Etienne, dressed all in black and with a cloud of white hair. She was very fastidious and correct. She had no clutter in the shop. I think that's maybe why I have a wall of tiny drawers now. I've never thought of that before. Anyway, there was a particular ribbon that Mme Etienne wanted to show us, but she realised she'd left it in her flat upstairs. So, taking us with her, she closed up, turning the open sign around on the door and then locking it. Once we were on the sunny, dappled pavement, she opened a tiny door next to the shop that I hadn't seen before. We tripped up dark stairs and entered the most extraordinary space. It was a vast salon with wooden floors, gilt mirrors and exquisite furniture. I remember gasping at the lavish curtains. But of course, now, thinking back to her professional interest in ribbons and all matters haberdashery, I'm not surprised. The curtains were light-coloured; beyond their swags, I could see a tiny balcony over the street. I felt as if the whole flat were a stage set, and that something dramatic and delicious was bound to happen there. We didn't stay for long. Mme Etienne quickly found the ribbon she needed and gave a sample to Deborah. On the way out, we shook hands with Mme Etienne. There, in her hallway, was a bunch of pink roses, and I remember the smell of what I imagine to be cooking soup coming from a tiny galley kitchen just next to the front door. I remember thinking then that I would love to live there. Strangely, I have been thinking more and more about that flat and wondering what happened to it and if it would be sold with the shop (were it ever to come on sale), and whether the shop still sells ribbons. When I told Judith about it, it made me realise that I had been dreaming about the flat, a sort of deep-down yearning for it. As if life would be so much simpler if I lived in that flat. Maybe you talking about Sarah's subconscious and her imaginary friend chimes with this. We are all fragile, aren't we?

Lots of love,
Anna.

24

Dear Anna,

We could do with you here at the moment. Dramatic curtains might be just the thing! Raggy has been so inspired by the boys' enthusiasm, that he has finally put into practice something he's been talking about for years. He always wanted to turn one of our outbuildings into a jazz venue. He'd got quite far with this before the trouble started with Sarah. At that point he abandoned his plans. So, it's good on all sorts of levels that he is starting to think about it again. And Sarah made him promise to let her do the interior decoration rather than call in a professional. I'm happy with that: the music room has never been right, and I dread to think how much we paid for that! And it gives Sarah a project, which can't be bad. Anyway, Raggy has got a phenomenal network of people who know how to do things, and this week we had in a lighting specialist, Jeff. Tobias has become his unofficial apprentice, and whenever I go into the barn, they always shout hello from somewhere up in the rafters. But it's coming on a treat. I can't believe the progress they've made. There's a proper stage area, hence my comment about the curtains, and there's space for dancing – unbelievably, they've been able to fit a sprung floor because another mate of Raggy's does floors, and then in front of that they've got tables and chairs that Raggy bought as a job lot from a venue that was closing down. Sarah seems to have commandeered Az to help her with the interior decoration. From what I can tell, she is going for a 1920s, Great Gatsby-inspired look. They're trying different colours on the walls, and at the moment seem to be favouring an eau-de-nil colour. They're always going off in the car to some shop that lets you mix your own colours. And that's really what I wanted to write to you about. It seems a bit simplistic now, but when Tobias and Az arrived, and Tobias was such a nice lad and about Sarah's age, I had hoped that they might become an item (cheeky: I do know he's your precious boy). He seems so sensible – perhaps that comes from never having had an imaginary friend! But I felt he wouldn't be spooked by Sarah's history with boys. He wouldn't stay away from her because of that, at the very least. They do certainly seem to be fond of each other. Tobias listens intently when Sarah speaks, and when she's quiet, he makes an express effort to bring her into the conversation. He notices what she wears. For instance, when the boys arrived, Sarah was wearing her habitual gym hoodie, with the hood up. When she took the hood down, Tobias commented that she had lovely hair. Sarah didn't put the hood back up and has even worn dresses instead of her gym uniform a couple of times. Tobias never fails to comment on how nice she looks, when this happens (don't worry, he's not being at all creepy). They are all tiny things, and perhaps I'm overemphasising them, but I really did hope they had an initial attraction to each other.

Now, I'm not so sure, though. We both know that Az is really dazzling. And it's not just his film star looks. He has that easy confidence that must come from knowing where he's going and what he's doing. He seems completely at home in himself, in a way that you wouldn't expect any seventeen-year-old boy like Tobias to feel. And, he seems able to turn his hand to anything – I've told you about the jazz piano – not sure where he learned to play, but Raggy sometimes shakes his head in amazement when Az riffs on a melody. Once they were rehearsing when I heard Raggy shout out to Az, 'Who taught you? Thelonious Monk?'

Az just smiled and carried on playing. But it's not just music. He's got this real sense of Raggy's vision for the jazz bar. He and Sarah returned from the paint shop via some second-hand emporium that I've never heard of. Sarah was trying to explain to me where it was, and although I know the general area, I can't say I really grasped her directions. She says it's a real Aladdin's cave. It's apparently run by a man whom I knew professionally. Once he retired as an Employment Tribunal judge, he started to do house clearances. Just for the fun of it! Brilliant! Do you agree with me about Wales, that it's sort of 'flat'; like there's no perceptible class structure as such? I suppose it's a bit like North America: anyone can be anything, I always think. It's almost like we've ditched a hierarchy in favour of a web... or something.

Anyway, whenever Az and Sarah return from the shop with the boot filled with lamps, large mirrors, even a bar, Raggy is thrilled. He always says it's exactly what he would have chosen himself. Az has even persuaded Sarah to paint some huge murals on the walls. And, amazingly, she has agreed! If anyone else had asked her, she'd have refused and put her hood up. But because it's Az, she thinks it's a great idea.

They've started sketching out these murals, and they are bigger than lifesize jazz age silhouettes of musicians and dancing couples. The man from the paint shop turns up occasionally to give them advice on brushes and colours. He has lent them some scaffolding, and they are always to be found scrambling over that, or locked in discussion at one of the bistro tables, heads down together over sketches for even more murals. They are completely wrapped up in each other, with jokes billowing through the barn. I watched Tobias watching them. Like me, he doesn't know what's going on. Az isn't leading Sarah on, but she hero worships him. It does me good just to write all this down, Anna (but don't get worried about Tobias, he seems curious rather than jealous, so far, anyway).

Kind regards,
Edna.

25

Dear Edna,

Thank you for your letter about the jazz barn. I was so inspired that I dug out an old CD we have of Miles Davis. His music swirled around the kitchen while I sat at the table with a cup of tea and scrolled through the local news. I'm glad I did, because there was a large piece about a craft prize. The National Museum of Wales is using some money to fund it. They want to make sure that creative industries are still supported here. So, there's a prize of £5000 for a piece of craft – and it can be anything – painting, sculpture, a piece of jewellery – anything – as long as it symbolises... you'll never guess what.... Music! Of course, I immediately thought of doing a wall-hung weaving with appliqué and embroidery, all jazzy; well, jazz-themed, anyway. What do you think?

I don't want to obsess, but we could really do with money sooner rather than later. I haven't quite got to the edge of the cliff at the shop yet, but I can see the waves slapping below (and it would be nice to have cash of my own, whatever happens with that credit due to T). If I got the prize, I'd buy a computer to keep all the records of what I have in the shop straight. At the moment, it's a bit like a lucky dip whenever the time comes to keep track with the wholesaler. It's not ideal, my haphazard method of bookkeeping! I always felt that my lack of organisation didn't help the fact that money from T was sometimes sporadic. But, somehow, it didn't seem to matter so much when it was just me and Tobias at home together. We didn't need much money to live on, and in any case, Deborah had made some wise investments. It's become much more difficult since T came back, though. I suppose that life is much more irregular now, and if I don't get round to opening the shop on a particular day – say I'm struggling with T's moods and he needs a bit of support – it stays shut. Which isn't really very good for commerce! And, while we wait for that credit to be collected (and we can't know the money is a dead cert in any case; so much time has gone by), then I'm sure that T must be eligible for some sort of benefit. But he refuses to engage with filling in the forms, and he had the cheek to tell me very sternly not even to look into what he's entitled to, because he won't claim it and then it'll only make me bitter. Somehow, he even manages to make his blindness my fault. Just imagine if I could win that money, all for myself!

I was thinking about this when T lumbered into the kitchen. He's put on weight, which is unsurprising, since he's sitting doing nothing all day. I don't know when he shaved last, even. All in all, he did look like an animal coming out of hibernation. Just now, he listened a moment to the music playing, and asked me blearily, 'Is that Miles Davis?'

And when I said yes, he just said, 'Well, well, well,' and lumbered back upstairs. In the old days, he'd have launched into a slightly bardic lecture about the genius of the musician. I used to listen patiently to these diatribes of his, feigning interest. I never thought I'd miss them. But, just then, I was glad he didn't stay in the kitchen, because my mind was full of the craft prize and I don't think I could have talked about anything else. It's best not to share what I'm thinking at this stage, anyway. I'll tell him later, of course, but for now I just want to let the idea of it percolate, and hug all its possibilities to myself. Well, except for telling you.

What you said about Tobias did make me smile. He is a good lad. I wouldn't worry too much about trying to get him and Sarah together. Although it might seem like a very good idea to us – I can certainly see the benefits from my point of view – it's got to be up to them, though, hasn't it? I often think how Deborah and Dai can't have thought I was the ideal wife for T. They can't have relished the prospect of this hippie daughter-in-law drooping around after their grandson. It would have been much better for his career if he'd married someone who was as driven and philanthropic as he used to be. Perhaps that person would cope better, now. Instead of just wading through each day and not seeming to get very far, as I'm doing. But whatever their reservations, they never showed me anything but courtesy and interest and love, yes, love. I think that has stood us in good stead. Although I would give anything to have Deborah here now – I feel so by myself, as if I'm at the end of a gangplank. Where is all this going to end, Edna?

Lots of love,
Anna.

26

Hi Anna,

You are the right wife for T! This is an exceptionally difficult time for you both, that's all. Wouldn't it be good if, after all this is over, your wall hanging ends up in our jazz barn? But, I suppose it only would if you didn't win, and I'm sure you will.

Funnily enough, the walls in the jazz barn *could* do with a wall hanging entitled, 'Jazz'. Just the thing! Sarah's murals do look a bit cold, I think. She and Az seem to be concentrating on scent at the moment. They want to fragrance the barn, I think, so that it smells exotic and rich. So, we've got joss sticks going with sandalwood and something citrussy. Az or Sarah will sniff meditatively as they go through the kitchen, and then add something to one of the innumerable petri dishes we seem to have covering every surface. (All this is driving Margaret mad, but Raggy is 'on a mission' with this jazz barn, so I've told Margaret to please just work round it.) I was in the kitchen yesterday, when Az came through and did the sniffing routine. I noticed him because, well, because he is Az. But, after he'd sniffed for a bit, he opened the freezer door and got out one of those little packets that the boys had brought with them – remember, the innards of the fish, or whatever. He untied the bag and put it to defrost in the microwave – the smell, Anna! – then, he held it above one of the petri dishes, so that its glutinous contents dripped slowly in. He watched intently the whole time. When the bag was empty and the whole room smelled foul (and it had smelt so good before!), he smiled. Although I didn't think he'd noticed me, he turned to me, holding the dish with the tips of his fingers and said, 'I'll just go and put this in Sarah's room.'

I don't know if it was a prank. I didn't think anything more of it. In fact, I'd forgotten it had happened until now. I must ask Margaret if she threw it out. Imagine if it spilt. That would be a real mess.

I could have asked Sarah, but she was on such good form this morning when she sailed through for breakfast, that I didn't like to rock the boat. She came into the room saying, 'I slept well last night. I can't remember the last time I slept so well.'

Perhaps because I didn't say anything, but just smiled, I looked at her more closely. She seemed clearer somehow, as if a weight had been lifted off her. She came to sit at the table, drinking coffee and intently peering at photos of the barn that she'd taken with her instamatic camera: pictures for her mood board, I guess. She spent ages moving them around and laying them partially over one another. Finally, she looked up and said, 'I've got it! I can see how this all fits together. I've got to go and find Az. Do you know where he is, Mum?'

And off she went, leaving me slightly non-plussed. I can't

remember the last time she called me Mum – for years now, it's always been 'Edna'.

Your boys have certainly shaken us all up!

Kind regards,
Edna.

27

Dear Edna,

I don't know much about aromatherapy. Sometimes I've been on taster sessions at courses I've been on. No one has ever mentioned using the innards of fish to enhance the smell. I am intrigued, though! I wonder what the boys are up to? I really hope they are behaving themselves. Don't let them get out of hand!! Seriously, it would be interesting to know what Az did, because it certainly seems to be linked to Sarah's suddenly feeling better – have you found out any more? Has Margaret been able to add any detail? I had a mad thought – don't laugh – I wonder if Az (as in Azariah) has got rid of As (as in Asmodeus)? All you say about Sarah seeming less preoccupied may mean that she's got less going on to worry about inside? Do you know what I mean?

On the other hand, I could be completely off beam – and if I am, blame sleep deprivation! I was up all last night finishing the wall hanging – I am pleased with it – I was surprised at how organically it grew. It helped to have music on in the background as I was doing it, and funnily enough, having a variety of music seemed to be good. So, I spent all my time hopping between radio stations in the shop. I do want to make sure the finished article gets there, now. And something about T makes me reluctant to leave him. He's become very quiet and tense. I realise that he's always quite quiet and tense these days, but this seems to be an escalation. So much so, that I can't bring myself to talk to him about the wall hanging. He seems so self-sufficient and internalised that my preoccupation with my wall hanging just seems irrelevant. Judith from next door has agreed to take the parcel to the post when I need to get it off to the prize people. I did enjoy packing it up. Long before online shopping, Deborah used to have a small mailorder section running from the shop – I used to love checking items off the list and making sure each was safely in the box, then writing the label and sending it away to somewhere I'd never been. It's funny now to think that I used to imagine I'd visit faraway places. The reality of travelling with T wasn't exactly my dream of exotic meandering and discovery, but I don't think that dream will happen now. Anyway, Judith breezed in to the shop and picked up the package this morning. Earlier, when I took T his breakfast in his room (because the latest thing seems to be a reluctance to come downstairs), I asked him if he wanted to see the wall hanging before I finally taped it up to send (I did eventually tell him what I was doing). I was quite proud that I'd made this tactile piece of art, so that it could be seen by touch. I wish I hadn't bothered to mention it to T, though. He just snapped, predictably, 'What do you mean, would I like to see it? Do you want to humiliate me even more? Don't you realise I don't care about your wall hanging? I don't care about what you do! I don't care about you!'

I couldn't think of anything to say. Even at his most exasperated, T has never talked to me like that before. So, I just backed out of his room. As I closed the door quietly, I could see that he had his head in his hands. I have never felt so cut off from him. I sat on the top of the stairs. Usually, I am the first to cry, but no tears came. It wasn't that I wasn't hurt but I was suddenly filled with the steely determination to carry on, no matter what. So, I went on my way and packaged up the wall hanging with real ferocity, cutting brown paper, slapping the package from side to side as I did up the twine and then jabbing on the address. I felt really defiant as I did it! And now we have to wait and see what the judges say.

Lots of love,
Anna.

28

Hi Anna,

I was thinking about what you said about Az and As; it does make sense in a funny kind of way. Suddenly, I felt very brave when Sarah came into the kitchen. I was sitting at the table looking through the weekend papers. I'm always concerned that I never get my money's worth from the library of weekend papers that arrive, and so they hang round for days afterwards. When I looked up, I saw Sarah still looking cleansed, somehow. She said, 'Have you seen Az?' I shook my head. 'Oh, I was hoping to catch up with him. There was one space on the wall in the jazz barn we were puzzling over and I think I might have found a solution. I'd like him to come and look at some pictures I found on my laptop. Will you tell him, if you see him, that I'm in the library?'

I took a deep breath and said, as disingenuously as I could, 'Oh, you mean the new Az, not the old As?'

Sarah turned round as she was going out of the kitchen. I have a clear picture of her framed in the doorway and looking genuinely puzzled, 'Who's 'the old As', Mum?'

I just waved my hand and let her go on her way. But I did sit there for quite a long time, cradling my coffee and wondering if

I'd imagined all those episodes with the malevolent imaginary friend. I was just thinking that it was time to move and do some job or other, when Az himself (the genuine article!) came in.

'Hello, Edna. Have you seen Sarah about it all?'

'In the library. But before you go, Az, may I ask you a really weird question?'

'Oh course.' He leant against the rail of the Aga. 'Weird questions are my favourite sort! Fire away!'

'I think Sarah's much better. Unburdened, somehow. I can't help wondering if you had something to do with it. For some reason, I seem to think the package of fish from the freezer in the petri dish is somehow mixed up in all of this. Am I losing the plot?'

Az roared with laughter and threw his head back, almost theatrically. For a moment, though, he looked like someone who had watched people finding things amusing on films and copied them, rather than someone who is genuinely amused. Oh, I don't know what I'm saying now. I suppose that, just for a moment, I had the feeling of someone playing a part. The really strange bit was that I didn't find this threatening at all, I didn't feel that we were in danger, any of us. Whoever Az is, he's one of the good guys.

'She is much better, isn't she?' he commented. 'I've noticed that. Maybe her being so keen on our plans for the jazz barn is taking command of whatever was making her sad before. I hope so. She's a good kid. She deserves to be really seen and understood. In the library... did you say?'

'Yes... but Az.... What about the petri dish?'

He waved airily, almost mimicking the wave I had given Sarah earlier.

'No, I just thought the ambient scent in the barn needed a bit more of a sour feel.' His face broke into a radiant smile. 'I think it did the trick, don't you?'

I was still smiling at the roguishness of his reply when he announced that he was going to be gone for a few days to pick up T's money. He didn't want to disturb Tobias, who seemed to be in the middle of some delicate operation with the sound or the lighting in the jazz barn, I forget which, but wondered if I'd let him know.

I sat there, watching his receding figure, wondering what the hell was going on, but somehow still trusting things would work out OK.

Kind regards,
Edna.

29

Dear Edna,

I won! I won! I've never won anything before in my life. The Lord Mayor's office contacted me yesterday by phone to say that my wall hanging had won first place. It'll be hanging in the mansion house – there will be a reception – and I'm invited. The prize money will be in my bank account in the morning. What a relief! I can't remember when I felt so energised by anything.

I was in the shop this morning before I opened up, just looking around and envisaging the changes I will make with the prize money. I wish Deborah could be here to advise me! But I must've been spinning around because I felt dizzy when I stopped suddenly when the doorbell rang. I could see through the window that it was the postman, who by that time was busying himself in his van, so I unbolted the door. I then saw that he had a box of flowers. I took them from him. I'm sure I was blushing, isn't that ridiculous? I carried them through to the kitchen and tore open the little envelope to get at a card announcing they were from the Mayor's office! I had just finished arranging them in the largest vase I could find. I was tearing the cardboard packaging into manageable strips when T came downstairs, unexpectedly.

'What the hell's going on?'

'I just received the most wonderful bouquet of flowers. Come here and smell them. There's roses and lilies. Every shade of pink you could imagine, T! It says that they were sent from Flowerz, that award-winning flower shop in town. You know the one where Judith's daughter did work experience? And, talking of winning awards....'

But here I was interrupted. T was leaning over the kitchen table, sniffing, but then I noticed his hands gripping the side of the table until the knuckles were white.

'Where have all these come from? Anna, are you having an affair? God knows, you'd be justified after all I've put you through, but, really, I thought you'd be more self-controlled than that! Is that what you've been up to behind my back? Is that why you were so keen for Tobias to clear off, so that you had no witnesses? And now your secret lover is sending flowers to your marital home. I can't believe you, Anna!'

For the second time this week, T had stunned me into silence. The flowers smelt sickly now and looked a bit pathetic in all their gaudiness. I was doing that thing I always do when I am challenged, I immediately diminish myself and demean what I'm proud of. Then suddenly I'd had enough of being some sort of browbeaten little woman. This time was different. How dare T jump to the conclusion that I was having an affair. I'm afraid I shouted at him. I said terrible things. I don't even like to think of them now, but I ranted about how righteous he enjoys appearing, how stupidly secretive he is about his work abroad – a UN project here, humanitarian work here – but all hush-hush, otherwise he'd be putting the lives of people on the ground in danger, how worthy of praise he likes to appear, how he enjoys people referring to him with awed respect. And all the time, he is thinking the most unworthy things. Well, I'd had enough. At that moment, I remembered the prize money coming into my bank account. That gave me confidence to say quietly, 'I've had enough, T. I need a break. I'll make sure you're taken care of, but I've got to get away for a bit.'

Without saying a word, he turned around, just shaking his head slightly, and made his way back upstairs. I started phoning Judith and those show-off flowers on the kitchen table just stared back at me.

Lots of love,
Anna.

30

Hi Anna,

Are you OK? But, before anything else, I've got to say 'Congratulations!' That's wonderful news! I had a feeling you'd win. You work so hard, you deserve it. Please let me know what the next steps will be? Will there be some sort of presentation? What will you wear? I think part of your prize money should go on buying a new outfit. You could go into the John Lewis in Cardiff. I'd offer to come with you, except that might be asking for trouble? We'd be seen and then it would all come out about how we'd corresponded. It doesn't take that much for misunderstandings to arise, exactly as it happened with that bouquet of flowers. I'm so sorry about that. That really is very unfair of T; I do hope that he feels duly bad when the truth comes out.

Talking of bad, there's a definite subdued quality to our life here at the moment. Az's departure seems to have taken the wind out of our sails. Although work is progressing with the jazz barn, it is all much more low-key (excuse the pun) than it was when he was here. I don't think I realised how much he was the Master of Ceremonies. He did say, though, that he'd be back as soon as he could after picking up the money, so it will be good to see him soon. Funny detail, though, he didn't want Raggy to drive him to the station. He said he'd walk; that he could do with the exercise. We all went out of the drive to see him off. After saying goodbye he walked up the hill, whereas the station is in the town centre at the bottom of the hill. We all yelled after him, Dorcas was running round madly and barking, and he reappeared at the end of the drive and gave us a thumbs up sign before going on his way downhill. How could he have thought that the train station was out of town? I was watching Sarah as we said goodbye. Her eyes were filled with tears. After Az had gone, Raggy and I turned to come back into the house, but Sarah and Tobias made their way back to the jazz room. As I shut the door behind us, I noticed that Tobias put his arm around Sarah's shoulder and they were walking quite slowly, quite contentedly. It was just what Sarah needed. Tobias is a good man.

I know you said 'don't think about it', but I'm still struck at how good it would be if Tobias and Sarah got together. He seems to understand her, intuitively. And from what I can tell when I see them together, he makes her happy. With Az, she was dazzled. I used to get the impression that when she was in his company she was always slightly squinting, as if his bright attraction was too much for her. By contrast, she and Tobias seem well matched. It would be a partnership of equals. But, you're right, you're right. It doesn't help to go on about it. It's funny who people end up with, isn't it? Whenever I've been surprised by the combination of husband and wife, I've realised that the choice of spouse can complement a part of their partner that's not dominant. I remember being at a Chambers' party once. A few members of our firm had been invited by counsel whom we used a lot. One of the barristers intrigued me. He was very eminent and flamboyant, although he always struck me as having low self-esteem, which he masked with bluster. I was shocked to see his wife. I think I'd expected a soignée 'trophy wife' type, but she was dressed all in black, in flat shoes, with short badly cut hair. She wasn't drinking or talking but going round as the unofficial photographer. I was perplexed until I saw the photos after. They were stunning. It was like she'd really seen people. No wonder he married her, her vision was so seductive. He'd have been able to rely totally on her judgment.

You've talked about Deborah not imagining you were the right wife for T. If she did think that, which I doubt, because you haven't really given me any evidence of it, I think she was wrong. With your enterprise and flair, you are just what T needs. But certainly, my family was alarmed when I said that Raggy and I were going on holiday and would be getting married while we were away. I think my parents were expecting some lavish wedding where they could invite their friends and show off their lawyer daughter marrying a suitable, professional groom. In fact, now I think about it, I don't think they'd even met Raggy properly. Maybe that was wilfulness on all our parts, not least on mine. He was certainly on the scene for a couple of years before we married, but I wasn't living at home then; I expect they thought that it was just a fad I was going through. I'd soon tire of a jazz musician with his erratic work and unsociable hours. But that's just it. Raggy was so different from anyone I'd met before. Our first date – if it was a date, which I doubt – involved going, in my car, to pick up and then take this stuff to a venue. It was wonderful. My other first dates had been like mini job interviews, but with Raggy, I suddenly felt on a different timescale. There would be plenty of time to find out all the details about him. Initially I was overwhelmed by how easy it was and how I felt so much myself. As I watched Tobias and Sarah going to the jazz barn, I was suddenly reminded of that.

Hang in there, Anna, and don't take too much notice of T! Oh, and congratulations again!

Kind regards,
Ed.

31

Dear Edna,

It wasn't that I was a complete cow. Before leaving, I went next door and rang on Judith's bell and got her to agree to go in and see to T on a regular basis while I'm away – get him food, make sure he's up and so on. She asked what she should tell him. I said I didn't care. I was beyond caring.

I was in such a state, I realised I hadn't put my watch on, but when I'd stepped into the road it was still early morning. I shivered and pulled my coat around me. Further up the road, I noticed the milkman. You can tell it's an up-and-coming area of Cardiff, we have the option of getting milk delivered! After speaking to Judith, I got the car keys out of my pocket. We have a very old, very yellow car. It used to be T's before we were married. I imagine he got it initially to be some sort of glaring statement against consumerism, because he always resents spending money on things like cars. I tend not to drive it when he's away and so it stays outside the house. I couldn't remember the last time I'd even been inside it.

Perhaps it's for that reason that I'm always struck by its smell. It smells as though something's growing in it, which to be fair, is probably the case. Of course, with that smell, came all the memories. Sometimes, I think I have a card index of memories: driving away into the darkness after our wedding party, T driving me and Tobias home from hospital, so I always seem to associate that vegetal smell with heightened emotion. My heightened emotion on this occasion was one of frustration, because the engine refused to start however much I turned the key and willed it to get going. It would be so awkward if T recognised the sound of the spurting car and came out of the front door to see what was going on. I leant back in the driver's seat and closed my eyes. When I opened them, I saw a huge black car stalking up the road in the early morning sunshine. Its throaty purr came closer. There it was, almost stationary, stopping at the intersection and waiting to see if any traffic was coming. And then proceeding on its way – majestically – a touch slowly as if it were looking for a house number. Then getting louder and louder as it progressed up the road. Until the sound stopped as the car braked when it was parallel with me. I looked over. There, gesticulating from the driver's seat, was Az.

'Get in,' he mouthed.

I shook my head, not in disagreement but in disbelief. As I got out of the yellow car, he pulled in and parked in front of me. I got into the passenger seat and looked over quizzically at him. But before I could say anything he had pulled out and was explaining, matter-of-factly, 'Do you want to come and help me pick up some money? I hope you do, since it's yours anyway!'

I didn't say anything, but looked over at his profile. He

was quite calm, as if it were the most ordinary thing in the world that we should meet and drive off together. He didn't take his eyes off the road and I had the oddest sensation, that he was discovering where we were going by seeing where the car took us. That's a mad thing to say; it is how I felt, though. He seemed so intent on watching where we were going, that I looked outside. I do love Cardiff. Those huge white civic buildings that look like they're made out of royal icing, and then the filigree spire of St John's Church and the castle, with its idealised façade. I always imagine that if a child were asked to design a castle, then you'd end up pretty much with Cardiff Castle. With its proper ramparts, painted figures in the tower, stone animals scaling the walls, even a drawbridge entrance and room for a portcullis, I've always found it such a satisfying building and never more so than this morning.

The car swung left, we cut through town, crossed the platitude of Callaghan Square and were on our way to the bay. The Millennium Centre was shining like a snoozing armadillo and there were fountains splashing, although no one was about to see them. The merry-go-round had not started up for the day and the seagulls were crying to each other that they had the Bay to themselves.

After parking the car on the ground floor of a multi-storey, Az and I walked across a zebra crossing and towards the main drag of shops. He still had the same intensity about him, as if he was looking for somewhere but wasn't sure of its name, like he'd know it when he saw it, or so he thought. He was dressed more carefully than I was, he'd obviously thought about the clothes he'd wear for this meeting. I'd only ever seen him in jeans before. He was always quite presentable, but this shirt, impeccably ironed and those brogues, carefully shined, made me think we were about quite a solemn business. His smile and his next comment belied this, 'It's a pity the ice cream shop isn't open yet. It seems ages since I had breakfast!'

We walked along the empty curved walkway between the sea and the built-up glamour of the shops and restaurants. It made me feel strangely amphibian, as if I were in a liminal zone between two realities. Suddenly I wasn't sure what was real. The early morning sunlight seemed to bounce off the grey waves that were coming in towards us, and I wasn't sure that I couldn't see the beginnings of, oh I don't know, another dimension. I started to feel unsure of myself. What was I doing? T would probably just be realising that I was not there when he shouted for me. Almost as if he sensed this, Az put his arm around my shoulder. I felt the weight of his forearm almost keeping me grounded. I looked over at him and smiled. He grinned back. There was no romance in his face; this was straightforward friendliness. I was hugely grateful, so grateful that I think I would have stopped and cried, had we not suddenly swerved to the left and entered a multiplex cinema.

I would have thought the door would be locked at this time in the morning, but when Az pushed it, it gave way. It was one of those new cinemas with chandeliers and sofas. There was no one at the welcome desk. The place seemed totally deserted. Az led the way to a lift, mumbling, 'I think it's the first floor we want.'

It was not one of those sleek new lifts, but rather it was a replica of the kind of lifts I'd seen in my childhood. It seemed very small, and there was a high perched stool in the corner nearest the buttons where, presumably, a lift attendant would sit. It was empty now and Az pressed the button. As the lift started to whirr and rumble, I caught Az smirking to himself. He involuntarily held the wall as the lift moved. I commented, 'Do you remember travelling in a lift like this when you were little? I remember one in a department store in the town where I grew up. I longed to work as a lift attendant. I thought it must be the most exciting job in the world.'

Az didn't answer. By then the doors were opening and he was looking for where he should go next.

'Oh there it is,' he said, referring to a door marked Staff Only. He rapped on it, comedically – Duh-duh-duh-duh, duh, duh, duh! – before opening it. It was a store room, with paper towels and bottles of bleach stacked tidily.

Suddenly, a woman's face peeped around the corner from where the sound of a boiling kettle was coming. She squealed when she saw Az and rushed towards him, 'Hiya, my love! I thought you might be visiting about now.'

She threw her arms around his neck and he embraced her warmly. He towered above her immaculately corn-braided hair and almost whispered, 'Lena, it's good to see you. You have no idea!'

Then he straightened up and held her at arms' length, saying, 'Is this your uniform, it's a bit of a change?'

She brushed her hands down the front of her brown

tabard and explained, 'Once I've finished my probation, they say they'll embroider my name on the front. I find I'm looking forward to that.'

'And Lena, what name is that?' asked Az.

'Lena Macsorley,' Lena answered in a matter-of-fact way. Then, noticing my look of bemusement, added quickly, 'But I was just making myself a cup of tea. Can you stop for one? What about you, love?' she asked, addressing me for the first time. 'You've had a very unusual day already. I bet you could do with a cup of tea.'

Az replied, 'We haven't really got time, Lena. Although a cup of tea with you would be lovely, we really should keep moving. Is the screen ready?'

'Yes, it is. I put some snacks out for you. I'll show you where it is. I'm just on my way to clean the loos at the end of that corridor.'

One after another, we backed out of the door. Az held the door open for Lena to manoeuvre her cleaning trolley out. We walked along and I was just thinking that, however swish multiplex cinemas are, they still smell the same, a combination of stale air and escapism. My thoughts were interrupted by Lena, 'Well, this is where I leave you.' She hugged Az again and said, 'It's been great to see you again. And you know where I am if you need me.' Then, she turned to me, 'It's been lovely finally meeting you... I know you'll make the right choice.' Then she squealed, 'Oh, I nearly forgot to give you this!' She delved into her trolley and brought out a large plastic bin bag. She opened it, showing the contents to me and Az – bank notes galore in massive denominations – before she pulled the drawstring handle and tied it up.

'Thanks Lena,' said Az, 'you're a star!' And they both guffawed, uproariously.

'Just doing my job!' she exclaimed as she went on her way. We turned into a darkened auditorium. As we looked at the cliff of seats, I could just make out that there were two towards the back which had side tables attached to them piled high with fizzy drinks, popcorn and sweets. We made our way there and sat down. I was just about to say something – I forget what – when the curtains in front of the screen opened. I'm trying to send this to you on my phone when I can. But things are happening pretty fast. Please bear with me.

Lots of love,
Anna.

32

Dear Edna,

I can't remember the last time I was in the cinema. For some reason, cinemas always seem to make me sad. I just remember irretrievable instances from the past when I'm there. There were times when T and I were dating, times when I took Tobias when he was little and he'd howl with laughter at cartoons, and then further back than that, the times when Deborah and I took Dai to the local arthouse cinema. This was before his final diagnosis but when he was starting to get distressed at losing his memory. But, the ritual of the cinema seemed to provide him with some solace. I'd never quite had an experience like this now, though. Az and I were the only people in the auditorium. There were no adverts, no announcement that the main feature was about to start, but suddenly the screen started to light up. I was acutely aware of Az next to me. As the screen flickered into life, he put down his fizzy drink and his popcorn, as if to attend properly. And then I felt his arm around my shoulder. I can't tell you the thrill of that. I turned to look at him. I couldn't see clearly but I imagined I saw a smile of such softness, as he kept his eyes on the screen, it was almost unbelievable. So, I sat there feeling perfectly secure, perfectly happy and somehow removed from all the anxieties of everyday life.

The screen showed a pavement. The light flickered through the leaves of the plane trees and there was that strangely comforting and unmistakeable sound of Parisian traffic. We were looking at a shop, it seemed to be selling stationery. Involuntarily, I sat forward – those are my favourite type of shops. I've sometimes thought of diversifying, so that my shop sells pens as well as craft stuff. The window was filled with pastel-coloured writing paper and there were matching cards and envelopes next to them. In the shop itself, I could make out the organised piles of writing paper and exercise books. It seemed to be doing a roaring trade. People were going in and out and then stopping to talk to the buxom lady behind the counter who had immaculately polished fingernails and that delicately coloured but severely cut bob that I always envy. Just then, I realised that I knew this place. It was where Madame Etienne's shop had been – yes, there were those beams in the ceiling that I had admired. The screen gave a wider view now and we were back on the pavement. Mme Etienne was no longer anywhere to be seen and in fact the door that had been the entrance to her flat had a For Rent sign attached to it. I suppose that's how things go. She had been a nice woman. I hadn't thought about her dying but of course she must have. I leant back to Az's arm which he pulled tight around my shoulder, almost as if he could sense my despondency.

The camera took us through the door and up the dark staircase. There, empty, was Madame Etienne's flat. I know I should have been distraught but, in spite of myself, I began mentally redecorating the empty space. I put a console table in the hall with a heavy vase filled with flowers on top. And a Delft jar on the floor for umbrellas. In the salon, I put swags of curtain and plenty of deep bookshelves. I scattered a medley of unmatched comfortable chairs around the room with strategically placed side tables. The walls were filled with art and treasures from travels. The windows were open and on the balcony I put a metal bistro table and chairs in very pale pink. Turning back towards the apartment and viewing it through the open doors, I decided the floors needed polishing, so brought those up to a bright warm sheen and placed some rugs – not too many – with muted colours through the apartment. I was just moving into the bathroom and was thinking about putting a row of plants that love humidity on a shelf when I became aware that Az was trying to say something to me.

'Would you like to live there, Anna?' he whispered.

'More than anything! But why are we whispering, we're the only ones here?'

He laughed and shook his head. Our faces were very close together. Az went on, 'If you want to go there, here's the key.' He pulled a large metal key from a pocket. It was attached to a tassel, heavy; the kind which Mme Etienne had sold. Perhaps it had been her key. It didn't strike me as bizarre that Az had it in his pocket in a multiplex. Rather, all my thoughts were concerned with Paris. Think of all I could do if I was there! At last, I'd be able to live! To live instead of simply waiting – waiting for T to come home, waiting for Tobias to grow up, waiting for the shop to make a profit, waiting for T's blindness to go. How would I earn money? Oh, I'd think of that once I was there. Perhaps there'd be a job in the stationery shop?

By now I was grasping the cool key in my palm and my fingers were wrapped around its shape. It felt like a talisman. I held my clenched hands up to my face and said earnestly to Az, 'Will you be there?'

Suddenly, that was what I wanted more than anything else: for Az, always so resourceful, always so light-hearted, to be with me all the time. What a life we'd have together! The two of us in an apartment in Paris. It would be wonderful to have someone there who seemed to know what I was thinking before I spoke. Imagine having that connection always. Being totally seen, totally understood, totally appreciated.

Again, Az laughed and shook his head. 'Oh I would love that, Anna. Believe me, I would like nothing more. But I'm afraid I can't. And the worst of it is, I can't tell you why. But you just have to trust me. It's ridiculous isn't it? I can produce the key for an apartment already waiting for you in Paris, and yet I can't justify why I can't do what I want and start a new life in Paris with you.'

And then, when I wasn't expecting it, he leant over and kissed my mouth very softly, very quickly. And I knew that that conversation was over.

'Come on,' he continued, as if nothing had happened. 'You don't need to decide right now. As long as you have made your decision by the time we get back to the car, that'll be plenty of time.'

The next thing I remember is the smell of fresh air as we exited the multiplex. I must have been deep in thought and I am only now imagining Az piloting me out. I remember looking at him, he no longer had his arm around me and I felt a sudden need to try and memorise him.

'Az,' I shrieked, 'the money! Where is the black plastic bag?'

He gasped, 'I left it in the cinema!' His eyes wide with the adventure of it all. 'Give me twenty seconds and I'll be back!' Lot going on, Edna... will be back to recap soon.

Lots of love,
Anna.

33

Dear Edna,

Sorry for this flurry of communications! No sooner do I finish writing than something else strikes me, which I simply must tell you. Speaking of which – another strange thing when we walked out of the cinema was that it was evening. The sun was setting and the shadows of all those crazily roofed buildings were filling the pavement. Az returned, laughing and clutching the black plastic sack. And so I didn't mention how strange it was that we'd entered the multiplex in the morning and come out so much later.

'I'm starving!' said Az. I suddenly realised that if it was evening, then I hadn't eaten all day. The smell of fish and chips was wafting towards us seductively and we gravitated towards a huge glass window. We sat at a table looking out, with plates each of fish and chips and slices of bread and butter and cups of tea – proper old-fashioned fish and chips. Cardiff Bay was still eerily quiet. There were very few people about: a solitary dog walker, a man cycling home from work late and cutting through the area.

'So, what happens now?' I asked Az. It was pathetic to be this out-of-control. I would do whatever he told me.

'Are you sure you want to go to Paris? By yourself, remember, I can't come with you.'

'Yes. I could become something there. There's nothing for me here....'

He didn't try and persuade me or question my reasoning. He just said, 'Right. Your suitcase is packed in the boot of the car. There's a plane leaving from Cardiff airport in three hours. If we drive straight there, you'll make it. You've got the key and here is a credit card which has some money on, but I'll put this into your account (he nudged the black plastic sack with his foot) in the morning. Oh, and your passport is in the glove compartment. Unfortunate photo, it strikes me. I think that's everything. Have I forgotten anything?'

'This is like a wonky version of *Casablanca*,' I commented. Az looked nonplussed. Amazed that he couldn't grasp the likeness between our situation and the Bogart/Bergman vortex, I blurted out, 'I'm still not sure why all this is happening. Why me? Who are you, Az?'

He replied calmly, 'I wish this could be the beginning of a beautiful friendship, Anna, but it's not, I'm afraid. I'm not allowed to tell you any more at the moment. You will have to trust me. I thought you trusted me?'

'I do, but you've got to admit all this is a bit seismic. If I'm in Paris, what will happen to T? What will happen to Tobias?'

'I really can't help you with any of that. I'm so sorry. You do have to make your own decision.'

Can someone listen gently? Looking over at Az as we finished our fish and chips, that was how he looked. He was listening gently, non-judgementally. He reached his hand across the table and covered my own. When I looked up at him, he was smiling, 'I don't want to rush you, Anna. But we haven't got unlimited time.'

I felt very silly. Here I was, agonising about a decision when it seemed that really there was no decision to be made. T would be fine, he always was. His pride would be hurt, but I wasn't really part of his reality. Helpers would flock around him. Tobias was away. He wouldn't come back and I wouldn't want him to. He's got his own life to lead. And I was being given the chance to flourish on my own terms.

'Paris,' I said quietly, 'definitely Paris.'

'So, you'll always have Paris then,' Az commented.

'OK, that's not even funny, Az. How do you do this stuff? I'm amazed that you don't frighten me. Let's go, now while the going's good.'

Az let go of my hand and pushed his chair back. This time he picked up the black plastic bag carefully and we sauntered back to the car. Suddenly, the questions in my head stopped. A calmness descended. I looked at the evening sunshine. I didn't want to remember all this as a dream. This was the most exciting, the most real thing that had ever happened to me.

When we got into the car, I opened the glove compartment. Of course, my passport was there. I picked it up. It was inside a cover that Tobias had made when he had still been in primary school. He'd had some idea that the passport itself had to really tell people who I was. He wanted the cover to explain my identity. You had to open the passport and put it facedown to be able to see his designs which ran over the back and the front. He'd drawn me and him close together and T a little way apart. Tobias and I seemed to be cooking something. The drawing was very intricate and I couldn't completely make it out in the dark of the multi-storey car park. There were Deborah and Dai. Dai was in the garden picking apples, which I suppose is one of the only memories Tobias must have had of him. And Deborah was sitting and looking on. I always associate her with activity, but it's interesting that Tobias seemed to remember her stillness. Holding it all together. There was her shop. There was the slide in the playground near the house. Isn't it funny how essential children's drawings are, cutting to the essence of personality and activity? There was one building that I couldn't make out at all: it seemed to be a sort of shiny dome. I gave up and looked at where we were driving. There, in front of us, inevitably, was a shiny dome. Of course: Techniquest, which had been Tobias' favourite destination for years. A hands-on science centre in the bay where kids could rush around screaming and doing experiments. There'd be a convocation of children every half hour to watch a demonstration. He loved it. I got ready to put the passport in my bag then caught sight of his drawing of Dorcas. Tobias seemed to have caught her way of moving in little more than a line drawing. She was jumping up – and yapping too, no doubt – as if she wanted to be included in whatever was going on. It was amazing! He must have observed her so closely. Then I thought – who would feed Dorcas, once Tobias brought her home? I gasped. No one else would know how you had to mix the food and only give her three quarters of the portion at first, filling up her bowl later. No one would know! I mean, she was fine for the time being as long as she was with Tobias, but what about when they came back and then Tobias went on his way without her. T had no knowledge of the Dorcas food routine and I hadn't told Judith. I couldn't go away and leave Dorcas like that. What if Tobias had come back today and dropped Dorcas off? This struck me as the most monumentally important detail in the world. The panicked look on my face must have been out of all proportion to the detail of feeding a dog who probably wasn't even in the house. But this didn't stop me from almost screaming,

'Home! I've got to go home!'

'Sure?' twinkled Az – and I had the strangest sensation that he'd almost been waiting for this. I nodded and the car turned back at the next roundabout towards the town centre. Phew! This is going to take some time to process....

Lots of love,
Anna.

34

Dear Anna,

So that's why Az arrived at the party late! Your marvellous, strange communications explained it all. I can't get my head around all you've told me to be able to comment; all I can do is take up the story. It was nearly midnight before Az appeared. He walked in and was a bit out of breath. I remember thinking he must have walked from the station – there was no sign of the car you talked about. There is much more to him than meets the eye, I certainly agree with you on that point!

He hadn't missed much. Although there had been dancing and supper, the proper inauguration of the jazz barn didn't start, I think, until about the time Az got there. He wouldn't dance. In fact, come to think of it, he looked a bit tired because I looked at him and asked, 'Long day?'

He answered, without really answering, 'Really good day. And I've got the money for T.'

'You haven't left it in the house, have you? There'll be so many people traipsing through there this evening, it would be hard to keep track of it.'

'No, it's already in their bank account.' There was certainly no sign of a black plastic bag anywhere. I do wonder how all that worked. But I suppose as long as the money is in T's account, I don't need to worry.

I stood next to Az as we watched the dancing. Sarah and Tobias had been dancing together all evening. They did look good together. Sarah's dress seemed to catch the spots of light from the glitter ball and it seemed to me that they were whirling around together in a pool of light. Raggy and his band were really in the zone. I've seen them play so often, I think I can sense when things are going well. The indicators are almost imperceptible: one instrument might echo another playfully, or two band members might exchange a glance. But it seemed effortless, then, as if there was total communication.

I got the feeling that Az would prefer to be left alone. I thought I was silly thinking this, but now I understand a bit what a strange day it must have been. He must have had a lot to think about. Perhaps that's why he suddenly looked very old (I know how improbable that sounds) and as if the very art of breathing – in, out, in, out – was enervating and laborious. He took a deep breath before engaging in conversation, 'It works – the jazz barn. It works.'

'Yes, doesn't it! Raggy has great plans and is already working on an opening season. We must add you to the mailing list. It would be wonderful to have you here as a regular, even when you no longer live with us, which won't be for a long time, I hope.'

'Mmmmm,' Az responded meditatively. Before he could answer properly, Raggy had stepped forward to the microphone.

'I'd like to play you something that I've been working on.'

There were whoops from the dance floor and the surrounding tables. Raggy nodded in acknowledgement and continued, 'It's called "That is not come to me which I suspected".'

'What?' was the uniform cry.

At that moment, Az handed me his beer and cupped his hands around his mouth. He shouted, '"That is not come to me which I suspected"! Excellent title, Raggy!' Az said this like it was a phrase he knew. Was it a private joke?

Raggy's face lit up when he saw that Az was back. I noticed Tobias and Sarah also turning towards him. Sarah waved to Az, but did not move from Tobias' arms.

'Come and play the piano!' shouted Raggy.

'No, you're doing just fine without me,' answered Az. 'And I don't know the tune.'

With that, Raggy turned back to the band and started playing this melody that I'd never heard before. And yet it was incredibly familiar. It was unlike anything that Raggy usually plays. It seemed to tell a complete story. No wonder it had that complicated title, because it spoke of someone being surprised by how simple everything is. They had assumed life would be complicated and filled by concessions and confrontation, but then, in the end, everything was straightforward. In that tune, I heard all our worries about Sarah, and our anxieties for her – that she would never be happy. Yet here she was with Tobias, swaying into the future in utter simplicity.

Kind regards,
Ed.

35

Dear Anna,

When Raggy stopped playing, amidst the applause, he extended his arm towards Tobias and Sarah declaring, 'Ladies and gentlemen, I give you Sarah and Tobias!'

The band played a fanfare and the dancefloor emptied around the couple, their shape together making an isolated elongated triangle lit up in darkness. They were leaning into each other and seemed to be on their own pedestal, forming their own slowly swaying statue. Tobias said something quietly to Sarah who nodded and hand-in-hand, they walked off the dancefloor, smiling. The band was playing background music and suddenly I noticed Raggy by my side.

'What's happening?' I asked him. 'This feels a bit formal, like they're getting engaged. Have I missed something?'

'Nope, we're just going with the flow, Edna. You should try it sometime,' he smiled reassuringly.

Sarah and Tobias didn't stop to say anything to us, they went on their way, completely entranced with each other. They walked out of the jazz barn towards the house, over the lawn, exchanging fairy lights for stars. As they approached the house, the security lights suddenly lit them up. Sarah was talking to Tobias who was listening attentively. We watched them in silence. And then I suddenly said to Raggy, 'Can you smell that?'

'No. What are you talking about, Edna? What should I be smelling?'

'There was some disgusting pot pourri that Az made Sarah a few days ago. I could just smell it again then. Are you sure you can't smell something funny?'

'I can't smell anything, Edna. Here's Az, you can ask him yourself.'

'Ask me what?' questioned Az.

'Oh nothing,' replied Raggy. 'Edna thought she could smell something, that's all, and I was looking to you to corroborate, sir, that there was nothing untoward in the air.'

'Nothing untoward at all,' said Az with solemnity, oblivious to the fact that Raggy was, well, ragging him.

'See,' said Raggy. 'I told you, Edna. Now let's eat, drink and be merry.' And with that, Raggy went back to the band, dragging Az with him. As they reached the stage, there were cheers when Raggy picked up his saxophone. He motioned the pianist to make way for Az and they started playing.

I looked out of the barn towards the house, which was now in darkness. And then I caught sight of something tucked away out of sight, but just inside the barn. It was a slim yellow plastic box, the size of a laptop computer. I stepped forward to investigate and could see written on the case were instructions about how to use the defibrillator within. I turned to look at Raggy on the stage – playing the saxophone as if nothing else mattered – but he had been thinking that this might be the night when Sarah and Tobias got together. He couldn't help remembering what had happened to those other lads. Good old Raggy. Just going with the flow, indeed. I smiled and swayed to the music.

Kind regards,
Edna.

36

Dear Anna,

This morning, Raggy, Az and I were eating breakfast together when Margaret came in and put her bag and coat behind the door, where she always puts them. It's quite a rare occurrence that different people are eating in the kitchen at the same time, well, for me, anyway. I'm always away before anyone else is up. It should have been a convivial atmosphere, but I think we were all quite hung over, not to say preoccupied. I never know in these situations if Raggy is simply oblivious to the tense atmosphere or whether he's just soldiering on with normality. He declared, 'Well, as Cole Porter almost said, "What a swell party it was!" It bodes well for the jazz barn. What did you think of the acoustics, Az?'

'I was pleasantly surprised. I thought that sound might get lost in the roof, but it seemed to be fine. Were you happy?'

'Yes. I thought the band sounded really energised there. I wonder if we could record in there. I'm thinking the acoustics are maybe up to that? But that's not a plan for this morning. I need to drink some more coffee first.'

'On my way,' muttered Margaret, She put the coffee pot down on the table as she prepared to start her work. I forget who it was from, but it is a very pleasing coffee pot. Somehow, it's pleasingness struck me this morning – beige, enamel. I do appreciate its low-key functionality. It wasn't trying to grasp at things it didn't understand, it wasn't worrying about consequences, it was just a coffeepot. Everything I'm not! Raggy picked it up, 'Do you want some, Ed?'

I nodded, smiling weakly. As he poured, he said, 'Are you all right? You seem very quiet. Didn't you enjoy it last night?'

'I thought it was marvellous. You all worked so hard to make the barn a reality. The evening was a triumph. I'm just a bit tired, that's all.'

Az twinkled at me. 'If you're worrying about Tobias, there's no need. I'm sure everything is fine.'

Margaret looked up from wiping a working surface, 'It is. They are. I went into Sarah's room when I arrived. The house was so quiet, I assumed you had all gone out, I didn't dream you were still sleeping. I saw Sarah and Tobias there. Although I had been very quiet opening the door, the movement roused Tobias and he looked over sleepily and raised his hand to me. I shut the door and tiptoed downstairs. And what about bacon sandwiches? You all look like you could do with some.'

So that was that. You'll be bloody relieved to know that your son is definitely truly alive!

Kind regards,
Ed.

37

Dear Edna,

Thank God!!! I knew Tobias would be okay! I just knew! Good job! I don't know how I managed to stay so unworried, but I had a very strong feeling when you were telling Sarah's story to me that none of it applied to Tobias – it wouldn't touch him. Call it a mother's intuition. It's so great, the way it's worked out for those two. But, I say that guiltily, because I haven't been thinking about Tobias or Sarah much at all lately. I seem to have been so preoccupied with myself.

When I opened the door on the evening I returned, the house was quiet. Then Judith came out from the kitchen – she raised her eyebrows to show she'd seen me, but I just smiled and shook my head. She then let herself out without another word and I was back. T had been in his room all day and hadn't really been aware of my absence, it seemed. I made myself a cup of tea and while I was waiting for the kettle to boil, looked over the sink into the dark garden. Everything was the same as before, the same as this morning when I'd rejected it all. There was the silhouette of the reproaching shed door, there was the grass that could do with cutting. Had I really chosen all this?

For a moment, I thought of the flat in Paris. I'd be putting the lamps on and busying myself in the smart kitchen, cooking with wonderful ingredients – fresh herbs, ripe fruit, soft cheese, crackly bread. No – this is what I have chosen. I had my chance and I rejected it. This was my reality, as rundown and empty as it seemed.

I was still musing on this when I heard T banging unsteadily down the stairs. He appeared in the kitchen and, in spite of myself, I smiled.

'Cup of tea?' I asked. 'I've just boiled the kettle.' To my surprise, he agreed, felt for a kitchen chair and sat at the table. I busied myself with the mugs and the milk. When I turned back around, carrying his mug to the table, I noticed that he was crying. He never cries but now his tears were plopping onto the wooden kitchen table.

'T, what's the matter?' I sat opposite him.

'I'm not sure. This sounds mad, but I had a sense that I'd lost you, yet here you are, back.' He paused. We drank our tea in the shadowy silence.

'I'm grateful, Anna. I really am. And then,' he continued, 'there's Tobias. I miss him. I think he may never come back. I've been trying to count up the days since he went, but I realise I haven't really got a grip of the time. I must do something about that. But he should be back by now. Is there some problem with the money?' He must have heard my forearm sliding across the table as I reached out to him, as he grabbed my hand. 'What if they haven't been able to find the place on the map? What if the money is gone? How will we live, Anna?'

I thought of Az's black plastic bag. 'I'm sure it'll be fine. Az is a good man and will sort everything out. They would have let us know if there was a problem.'

'I don't know,' he continued, pushing his hand through long hair that could do with a wash. Seeing him like that made me wonder if I was just being wafted away by the glamour of Az. Had I just been refusing to face up to my situation here?

'Perhaps you are right. After all, we know nothing about Az,' I said lightly. 'He could be a member of a cult. He might be brainwashing Tobias. He might be organising some complex way to feed us misinformation. Why didn't I think of this possibility before? Why did I just accept everything at face value?'

'Anna, what are you on about?' T replied. 'What's all this about feeding us misinformation? You always do this! I just want to talk through a problem and you end up mock-catastrophising and coming up with some alternative reality involving aliens taking over the world!' There was a smile in T's voice as he said this. I laughed, in spite of myself, and said, 'Aliens taking over the world.... That's a bit steep. But I'm just worried, T, when you're worried. I don't think you realise how much I lean on you and take your opinion to heart. If you lose hope, I lose hope.'

'Don't lose heart. I'm sure it will work out.' This sounded more like something Az would say than T. He didn't sound sure, though. I wish I could share with him what I knew, but then I wondered how much of what I knew was true. Was it reliable? These emails from you, even? The wonderful day with

Az? It all seemed frivolous and insubstantial. We sat there in the dark and the quiet, holding hands across the kitchen table, for a long time.

Lots of love,
Anna.

38

Dear Anna,

They are on their way to you, Sarah included! Get the bunting out! Raggy drove them all back to the station this morning. They were insistent that they didn't want Raggy to run them the twelve miles to your house. They were adamant – they had to travel by train. There was no sign of Az's large black car. To be honest, we could have done with it. The three of them had so many bags and then there was Dorcas yapping excitedly. It was only with a great deal of patience that Sarah could get her to go onto the lead. She was jumping up at everyone, as if she understood that the outcome to Az and Tobias' pilgrimage had been successful, on all sorts of fronts.

The black plastic bag was nowhere to be seen, so I did query, 'Have you got T's money?'

Az, who was lifting yet more bags into the car (all Sarah's art material had to be fitted in, for some reason) lifted his hand, reassuringly, 'I already said, Edna. It's in their bank account. You don't need to worry about anything!'

I don't know how long they'll be with you. But I got the feeling that for Tobias and Sarah, at least, this was a big departure. Sarah never went away to college. This felt like a student departure; one that is definitive. I mean it's a good thing that she's going, and home will always be back here when she needs us. Of course, I didn't say anything, but I did feel that this was 'for good' in all senses of the phrase. Hopefully, though, they won't be staying at yours forever!

There was much wedging of doors shut and beeping of the horn and waving. I stood watching them until they were out of sight. Then, I got into my car to go to the office. As ever, the car with its comfortable seats and subtle music and calming air-conditioning was a real benediction. I felt like I was rejoining the human race. For the first time in years, I wasn't shredded with worry about Sarah.

I do wonder what it will be like going back to the house this evening – very quiet, I should imagine. Margaret will have cleaned the rooms and changed the beds. So, everything will be in order. Raggy will have probably cooked the evening meal. Then I wouldn't mind having a look at the jazz barn. I don't feel I've caught up with all the developments there. I feel ashamed admitting that I don't envy you at all having that carful arriving (hope you have room for Sarah too)! But even so, I am curious to know how it all goes. Will you keep emailing? Oh, but Anna, I do want to warn you that our correspondence should still be a secret. I can't recall the number of times I almost blurted out, 'Anna said' or 'when I told Anna about this, she thought...'. It would sound so spooky, wouldn't it, to declare now that we'd been writing to each other and hadn't mentioned anything for all this time?

Oh dear, that sounds like an adolescent infatuation, doesn't it? But you know what I mean.

Having said that, it will be great to meet you. I'm sure that this bizarre time will all make sense, given a bit of distance. But for the moment it's just too close up for me to make any sense of it. Central to everything that baffles me about this is Az. Who is he, Anna? I had made up my mind to ask him, once and for all, before he left. But somehow, in all the rush of leaving, the opportunity slipped away.

Here I am going on, and yet the whirlwind is just about to make landfall with you. I'll leave you to it – oh that's great news about you and T – I'm so glad. When you get a minute, will you let me know how it's going?

Love,
Ed.

39

Dear Edna,

Thank you for the tip off! As soon as I'd finished reading your message I went and looked outside the front door. There, indeed they all were piling out of the station taxi. First Tobias who gave me a hug, although he nearly overbalanced because of the weight of his rucksack. Then Sarah, whom I kissed – oh, what a lovely girl she is, Edna – really straightforward. She exclaimed straightaway, 'Is that yours? A craft shop? That is a dream come true for me! Can I help you there?'

'Of course. I could do with all the help I can get. I've just won some prize money that I would like to spend on refurbishing it. It would be great if we could chat that through together. But for now, come inside, meet T and see your room.'

Lastly, Az, who let down a very over-excited Dorcas from his lap, got out. As he turned from paying the driver, he called out, 'Tobias, don't forget the ointment!' Tobias held up a small phial of liquid inside a greasy looking plastic bag, which made me think that it was perhaps the other bag of fish innards that had been in your freezer. I bet if you check, you'll find it gone. Tobias led the way into the house. Sarah was looking round, admiring our tiny front garden and Az linked arms with me, 'Are you okay, Anna? You've had a lot to process. More than anyone else can imagine.'

'I'm fine,' I answered. Az looked at me sceptically, expectantly, 'I'll be fine,' I corrected and he laughed as if I'd said the funniest thing.

Tobias was shouting, 'Dad, Dad – I'm home. We've got the money and I think I can help with your sight. We've created this ointment for you. Well, I say ointment. It's just the gall of the fish that Az and I bought. Will you try it?'

As Dorcas raced, yapping, from one person to another, I could hear T making his way downstairs. This was an incredible turn of events. I had no doubt that the ointment would work beautifully if Az had anything to do with it. With that, T came into the kitchen. He fumbled, 'Tobias is that really you? Are you really back? Let me touch you.'

Tobias stepped forward to hug his father, still clutching the phial with sticky fingers. And just at that moment Dorcas jumped up to T. Of course, T hadn't seen Dorcas coming and in his surprise, he put his hand out and knocked the phial of fish gall out of Tobias' grasp. It shattered on the floor and there was a terrible sound in the air of splintering and gasping. Dorcas sniffed the smelly puddle disdainfully. No one said anything, until T broke the silence. He took a deep breath, and I could tell that this was going to be vintage T. He'd thought everything through in a nano-second, weighed it all up and was about to deliver it eloquently.

He'd use exactly the same skills as he'd used to wheedle governments, raise funds, effect change. I braced myself. 'I've been thinking my blindness is a real inconvenience and of course I wish I could see again, but the blindness isn't really the problem. I'm not the only person who is blind. This has made me realise that I'm not unique. And I think that's the first time I realised that. I always thought I was special: it's laughable to think that that was my perception. But I suppose first Deborah and Dai tried to make it up to me for having absent parents, and then my work was so secretive and so dangerous. So, the cumulative effect was that I thought I was special. I couldn't see that the reality was not that at all. It was that I was supported more than I deserved to be. Tobias, you and your mother held the fort here while I was jazzing about overseas. Then, Az appeared just in time to go with you and get the money and your mother has been so patient with me. I haven't made it easy for her, I can assure you. And now, you come home with a beautiful wife.'

'Hey,' Sarah laughed, 'not so fast! And anyway, how do you know I'm beautiful?'

T laughed, 'Because anyone who can stop me from becoming too bardic is beautiful.' Tobias and Sarah stepped forward to hug T, and he went on, 'So can you see, the blindness is not the problem, I'm the problem.'

Vintage T. I looked over at Az, who leant down to retrieve a toy for Dorcas. He un-bent, smiling as he did so, 'If we are going in for the truth, the whole truth and nothing but the truth, I suppose I'd better come clean,' he mumbled sheepishly.

I bet you think we'll never get to the bottom of who Az is, Ed?

Lots of love,
Anna.

40

Dear Edna,

Az started by asking, 'What's that funny idiom you have? Killing foxes with sticks?'

'Birds with stones,' we all chanted, a bit perplexed.

'Yes. Idiom was never really my strong suit. Oh, "strong suit". I think I used that properly and I wasn't even trying. If only I was going to be here for a bit longer, I'm sure I could nail it.'

'Are you going somewhere?' asked Tobias, and Sarah almost involuntarily put her hand on his arm.

'Well... yes. It's probably occurred to you that I'm not totally at home in this reality. There may have been telltale signs, like not being familiar with idiom and I'm sure you'll think of more and more in the days ahead.' I felt myself blushing, Ed, at the thought of all the questions we'd asked ourselves about Az's identity. 'And the truth is that this isn't my reality. I'm not from far away. There are similarities and connections between these two dimensions – yours and mine, but this isn't home for me. I can't give you any proof, you just have to take my word for it, I'm afraid. I had hoped to get away without saying anything at all, that's what we're always taught is the ideal – to just disappear as easily as we appeared.

But, this time has been different; somehow, you deserve an explanation. I can only give an explanation of sorts. But it goes something like this. I'm from an organisation called The Network. That's the nearest word for it in your language. I think you may have other poetic names, and I think your religions specialise in those. The job of The Network is to keep everything in balance, to minimise waste. We don't want anything disposed of before its time, because that unbalances everything. I hope I'm not betraying confidences but T and Sarah came to my attention as being dangerously close to disposing of themselves, and that would have led, in their particular instances, to avoidable lop-sidedness. The Network can't always help in these situations, but I made the case that there was in fact a connection between your circumstances. I had a hunch that if I could create that link and give it more solidity, then the danger of T and Sarah throwing everything out of whack would go away. My job is what The Network calls "healing". You have that word too, don't you? Anyway, I am in the healing division. I think,' he added, looking around at us all, 'I was right to intervene, although not everything has gone to plan.'

Sarah started to reassure him, but Az raised his hand, smiling. 'It'll be OK, just rather a rigorous de-briefing process, I expect. And maybe it'll be a little while before my next mission.'

'This is sounding very like science fiction, Az. How much of it has been real?' asked T sharply.

'Oh, everything has been real, sir, but it's just that some

stuff may have been more real than you're used to. I'm sorry I can't explain fully but I promise you that you will understand. For the moment, it would be great, and it would really help me, if you accepted that the money is real and that the new connections you've made are real and that your differing perspective and fresh insights are real. Could you do that?'

Az looked at each of us in turn. He called us each by name, like he was taking a register. He even included Dorcas, who barked obligingly.

Tobias looked like he couldn't help himself when his turn came and he asked, 'Is your name really Az?'

'No. I wasn't always very good at answering to Az, perhaps you noticed, particularly when I was tired. I shouldn't really tell you my Network name, but I'm sure it can't matter now. Anyway, it's Raphael. That identifies me as being in the healing division. And now I really should be going.'

'Is there anything you want us to do?' I asked and realised as soon as I said it that it was a stupid thing to ask. But I was so far out of my comfort zone, that I didn't care. It seemed to me that I was doing anything to keep Az with us a bit longer.

'Oh, Anna. I think it's been harder for you than anyone. You came so close to realising the truth about me. But I just couldn't let you know. It would have put the whole mission in jeopardy. What you can do now is stop worrying. It will go well with you, I give you my word. Is that OK?'

It's ridiculous, I know. But, somehow I felt emotional all of a sudden, and it wasn't about Az leaving. It was as if the truth was setting me free. And I felt tired, very tired. I could feel my eyes filling with tears and I was desperately trying to hold them back when Az, or Raphael or whoever he is added, 'I'll let myself out. If you could all stay here till I'm gone I think that would be best.'

'But,' I started, still hoping to keep him with us, 'is that it? How are we going to talk about this? How are we going to make this strand fit the fabric of our lives?'

He was undeterred. There was no stopping this man – this being – although he smiled as he said, 'Ever the crafting analogies, Anna! But it might be an idea,' he mused, as if he wasn't really thinking of an answer to my question but his mind was already racing towards what was in front of him, 'to write down everything that has happened in a book. I leave that with you, Anna. I think you and Edna might have some notes in draft already?'

With that, he looked at each one of us again, as if he was trying to commit us to memory. With a wave of his hand, he left the kitchen and went towards the front door. None of us followed. We stood there, transfixed, and heard the front door open and close, followed shortly by the unmistakeable purring of the big black car. We listened to the noise of the receding engine, as though it was the last notes of a symphony. After it had well and truly disappeared round the corner of the road, Sarah said, 'Shall I put the kettle on?'

Lots of love,
Anna.

ACKNOWLEDGEMENTS

With gratitude to all the angels who have been passing.

SPECIAL THANKS

Special thanks are due from the publishers to Richard Powell, our philanthropic sponsor in the New Welsh Writing Awards manuscript prize, which has greatly benefited from this ongoing generous annual support.

A New Welsh Writing Awards winner, originally created
by *New Welsh Review*.

NEW
WELSH RAREBYTE